"I'm *Not* Wearing A Tuxedo."

"I can understand how you feel, Wade, but it's your only child's wedding."

"I'll give Myra Jo the full three-ring circus, but I won't play the trained bear for anybody. I'm no weekend cowboy, Leah, thinking I'm a rancher because I own a few acres and run a few head. I work my land and my herds. My hands get dirty and my boots aren't for show."

Wade suddenly looked weary, and Leah felt her heart pull. Whatever the reason, it was clear a battle would wage to put some shine on a man who wore his humble beginnings like a badge of honor.

"So...have I scared you off?"

"Nope." She held out her hand. "You may have met your match...."

Dear Reader,

THE BLACK WATCH returns! The men you found so intriguing are now joined by women who are also part of this secret organization created by BJ James. Look for them in *Whispers in the Dark,* this month's MAN OF THE MONTH.

Leanne Banks's delightful miniseries HOW TO CATCH A PRINCESS—all about three childhood friends who kiss a lot of frogs before they each meet their handsome prince—continues with *The You-Can't-Make-Me Bride.* And Elizabeth Bevarly's series THE FAMILY McCORMICK concludes with *Georgia Meets Her Groom.* Romance blooms as the McCormick family is finally reunited.

Peggy Moreland's tantalizing miniseries TROUBLE IN TEXAS begins this month with *Marry Me, Cowboy.* When the men of Temptation, Texas, decide they want wives, they find them the newfangled way—they *advertise!*

A Western from Jackie Merritt is always a treat, so I'm excited about this month's *Wind River Ranch*—it's ultrasensuous and totally compelling. And the month is completed with *Wedding Planner Tames Rancher!,* an engaging romp by Pamela Ingrahm. There's nothing better than curling up with a Silhouette Desire book, so enjoy!

Regards,

Lucia Macro

Senior Editor

Please address questions and book requests to:
Silhouette Reader Service
U.S.: 3010 Walden Ave., P.O. Box 1325, Buffalo, NY 14269
Canadian: P.O. Box 609, Fort Erie, Ont. L2A 5X3

PAMELA INGRAHM

WEDDING PLANNER TAMES RANCHER!

SILHOUETTE *Desire*®

Published by Silhouette Books

America's Publisher of Contemporary Romance

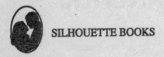

SILHOUETTE BOOKS

RECYCLED PAPER

ISBN 0-373-76086-8

WEDDING PLANNER TAMES RANCHER!

Copyright © 1997 by Paula D'Etcheverry

Printed in U.S.A.

Books by Pamela Ingrahm

Silhouette Desire

Cowboy Homecoming #964
The Bride Wore Tie-Dye #1038
Wedding Planner Tames Rancher! #1086

PAMELA INGRAHM

lives in Austin, Texas, with the man of her dreams and their two children. She's added to the mix one dog that thinks the human race was put here to love her, and Pamela swears she's not doing anything to foster that notion. She also tells all who will listen how wonderful it is to live your dream.

One

"Has he been by yet?"

"Nope," Leah Houston answered her partner, hoping Rhonda missed the nervous jump the mere mention of *him* evoked. She kept her eyes on the new publicity photo for Brides and Babies, her business and her pride and joy.

"What's that?" Rhonda set down the soft drinks she'd just purchased and straightened the curtains separating the little storage area where they sat from the display area. The strips of satin hid the paraphernalia they had transported from the boutique to the convention center for the bridal fair.

Leah took a grateful sip of cola and dabbed a bead of perspiration from her forehead. Although the convention center was air-conditioned—something of a necessity for Austin in June—she was still feeling the effects of the heat.

She handed over the photo to Rhonda and waited. Brides and Babies was her brainchild, and she had nurtured it from a one-person operation to its present staff of nine. Rhonda had been with her the longest—six years now—and covered the "and Babies" side of things.

"This will look wonderful on the new brochures," Rhonda said as she cocked her head sideways, making the long, silky blond hair Leah would have given her eyeteeth to have cascade off one shoulder. "Your dad would be so proud."

Leah managed a smile. Her father had died when she was twelve, but even at that young age he had instilled in her the need to "be" someone someday.

"I hope so. He wanted so much more for himself, but with my mom having kids every eighteen months, or thereabouts, he had to work two jobs to keep a roof over our heads. I think he had dreams and passed the torch to me."

"You certainly ran with it. Of course, when you came up with the cockamamy idea of putting a baby boutique around the corner from the bridal shop, I thought you were a certifiable lunatic."

"Thanks for the rousing vote of confidence."

"I hate to admit it," Rhonda confessed, "but it was a good thing you didn't listen to me."

"I listened," Leah protested innocently. "I just didn't pay attention."

Rhonda rolled her eyes and shook her head despairingly, but in the next moment all teasing was gone.

"You *are* going to take the Mackey wedding, though, aren't you? I mean, you've worked with Myra Jo before, so you know she'll be fun. And you have to admit, being around her sexy, single daddy would have some…interesting…advantages."

Leah grimaced. "I don't have to admit any such thing, and Wade Mackey's sexiness is irrelevant. I have to weigh whether this wedding is going to repair my reputation or damage it further."

"Oh, come on! You've only lost three weddings since the Robertson fiasco. And, I might add, you didn't make Penelope Robertson walk out of her own wedding."

"No, but her mama sure let everyone think I'd upset Penelope-poo so much she had to leave the church."

"So she made you a scapegoat. The weddings that went south were worth losing, if the people believed those stupid rumors. Besides, you haven't exactly had to declare bankruptcy. 'Babies' is doing a great turn this quarter, so quit worrying."

"I can't be as casual about this as you are, Rhonda. This business is my life, and I take those lost contracts personally. The money isn't the issue. My reputation is."

Rhonda put a perfectly manicured hand on Leah's shoulder. "Forgive me for being flippant. No one knows more than I do how hard you work. I guess that's why I don't understand your reluctance about the Mackey wedding."

Leah gave her friend an incredulous look. "You're kidding, right? The bride's daddy is a well-known rancher who hates politicians, and the groom's daddy is the most well-known senator in Texas. If those two men go after each other, it'll make the Robertson affair look like a cakewalk."

Rhonda tried to be positive. "Surely they wouldn't do anything foolish at a big wedding."

Leah shook her head. "Experience has taught me that the bigger the opportunity for disaster, the greater the chance for abominable behavior."

Leah took another sip of cola and listened as the vendors around them dismantled their stalls. The noise distracted her, making her think about the job ahead of her. She'd hired a textiles major from the university to arrange her booth, but she'd decided to save money by taking the stall down herself. Even with Rhonda's help, she wasn't looking forward to the next few hours.

Voices from beyond the curtain caught her attention.

Leah felt sure the deep one belonged to Wade Mackey, and was irritated by her pulse's response.

She never allowed anyone to interfere with her business, and she was frustrated by Wade Mackey's failure to follow the rules. She'd only met the man once, but she'd had to remind herself constantly since the Griffen wedding that she was not interested in lean, dark cowboys with disconcerting gray eyes. The lean and dark were fine, even the gray eyes were fine, but she had no interest in a swaggering, overbearing cattle baron.

Her conscience scolded her. Nothing about Wade Mackey supported her choice of adjectives. Confident, maybe, but hardly swaggering. Assertive, maybe, but hardly overbearing. He was the kind of man a woman could depend on, snuggle close to and feel, just for a moment, as if she wasn't alone.

Quieting her conscience, she checked to be sure no hair had escaped her sleek chignon. She most assuredly didn't need a man's protection. She'd been dating Brandt off and on for almost three years now, hadn't she? And she certainly didn't feel protected when she was with him. She'd made it to the advanced age of thirty-five on her own, thank you very much, and if she needed security, she'd buy a guard dog.

Straightening her suit—her favorite as it did wonders to hide her hips—Leah stepped into the display area.

And nearly stumbled. Even though she'd been expecting him, she must have forgotten just how right Rhonda could be at times. Handsome was an understatement.

He was tall, Texan tall, at least six-two or -three. His shoulders looked broad enough to battle a reluctant calf, or maybe a dragon, or to support a woman's tired head. His arms were hidden beneath the soft cotton of his shirt, but she remembered the steely strength in his fingers, even though his grasp had been gentle. She didn't dare glance down at the hips she knew were narrow or the thighs hidden beneath the denim of his jeans. Just the memory of him in slacks and a sports jacket was enough to make her light-headed.

The beautiful girl at his side was his daughter, Myra Jo. The gossips had been tripping over their figurative tongues to give the juicy details of her courtship with Pennington Bradford, son of the wealthy and powerful Senator Johnson Bradford.

"Mr. Mackey, Myra Jo! How nice to see you again. Welcome to Brides and Babies," she said to announce herself.

"Ma'am," he said, nodding as he switched the straw cowboy hat from his right hand to his left so he could accept her handshake. "And please, it's just Wade, remember?"

How could she forget? The memory of Tammy Griffen's wedding, and of his fingers against hers, came back in a powerful rush. She remembered how she would turn at the oddest times and find Wade's eyes on her. She had hated knowing his penetrating gray gaze had pierced the shield of her professionalism. He had flustered her the entire evening.

Pulling her attention away, she clasped Myra Jo's fingers warmly. "Best wishes on your engagement. I hope you and Mr. Bradford will be very happy."

Myra Jo tossed her a cheeky grin. "Mr. Bradford's already happily married, but Pennington and I plan on proving all the doomsayers wrong."

She cast a quick glance at her father before returning innocent eyes to Leah.

Leah chuckled, remembering Myra Jo's quirky sense of humor from the usual prewedding ruckus in the bride's lounge. She had kept Tammy Griffen laughing so hard she hadn't had time to be nervous.

"You were a good friend to Tammy. She made it all the way up the aisle without tripping. That girl was—"

"A hoot?" Myra Jo interjected.

Leah's answering smile widened, despite her best effort. "A good choice of words, I think."

Myra Jo tucked her palm in the curve of her father's arm. "I think Tammy picked those awful bridesmaid dresses just to make us look goofy."

Leah was grateful Tammy had not chosen her attendants' gowns at Brides and Babies—not that her shop would have ever carried such monstrosities—because Myra Jo was right. The hideous burnt orange satin had made the girls look like something out of a Halloween nightmare next to their black-clad escorts.

"You were awfully good-natured about it," Leah said, trying to be diplomatic.

"What could we do? It was her wedding. If she wanted seven pumpkins walking down the aisle, who were we to argue?"

A full-throated laugh burst from Leah. Again, Myra Jo was correct. The little hats Tammy had chosen, with a net veil and a green feather perched on the side, had indeed made the slender bridesmaids look like marching veggies, except Leah thought the girls had looked more like carrots than pumpkins.

Myra Jo gave her father's arm a little shake. "Daddy had the bad manners to laugh when he saw us."

"I pretended to cough," he defended himself, his deep voice laced with humor.

Leah kept her smile frozen in place as a flash of agitation coursed through her. She distinctly remembered the clenching in her gut when she'd searched the crowd for the unmistakable sound, knowing somehow just who was jeopardizing months of her hard work. Her own desire to laugh hadn't eased her resentment. It was one thing to think of laughing and another to do it.

Before she got good and angry at the memory, she looked back at Myra Jo. She was a younger, decidedly female version of her father, with the same aquiline nose, the same full lips, the same high cheekbones. Her ebony tresses were swept back from her delicate face in a loose French braid trailing down her back. Leah suspected Wade's midnight hair, cut short against his well-formed head, would curl defiantly if left to grow.

Myra Jo had none of her father's tall ruggedness, though. She was barely five-one, and looked so fragile a strong wind might blow her over. Leah noticed faint smudges under the girl's eyes, despite her perfect makeup. If she had to guess, and since she did so regularly, she would put Myra Jo at a size six.

"So, what can I help you with today?" Leah asked, bringing the subject back to business. People were walking past with boxes and crates, and it was going to be hard enough to keep their attention while the place was being torn down around them.

Myra Jo withdrew her arm from her father's and clasped her hands together. Her expression tightened just enough to make the shadows under her eyes seem deeper.

"Well," Myra Jo cleared her throat. "Just about the only thing Daddy and I haven't fought about is asking you to do the wedding. I've pushed the date back twice for Daddy, but this time I've already reserved the church and sent out my invitations."

"The problem," Wade interjected, "is that now she's only given herself a month to get all the rest of the details put together."

To Leah, Wade's irritation with his daughter was almost palpable.

"Anyway," Myra Jo continued, "Daddy thought you did a great job keeping the 'Hatfields and McCoys' apart at Tammy's wedding, so if anyone can referee the ten rounds until Penn and I get married, and maybe get my bullheaded father into a tuxedo, it's you.''

Leah cast an astonished glance at Wade. She wasn't surprised Myra Jo was interested—they'd gotten along fabulously at the Griffen wedding. But to know Wade approved of his daughter's choice based on a brief introduction at the reception was more than a shock. She was hardly an expert on Wade Mackey, but she didn't see him as the impulsive type.

"Thank you for your confidence. I'll try to do my best for you." *I just hope I don't regret it.*

Myra Jo patted her father's arm. "I'm going to run down to that honeymoon packager before they close. I'll be right back."

"Wait—"

But she was gone. Wade shook his head.

"Kids," he said, shrugging one shoulder.

"She's lovely."

Pride radiated from his whole body. "Thank you." He turned his head to watch Myra Jo's retreating figure. "But sometimes she's the most stubborn cuss I've ever met."

"She must take after her father," Leah said straightfaced.

Wade's glance darted back to her, and the corner of his mouth twitched. "I've heard a similar suggestion once or twice."

She should have won an Oscar for the innocence of her expression. "Still, I'm looking forward to working with her."

"Then let's hope you enjoy her father just as much."

He delivered the words in a quiet, warning tone. Leah didn't feel intimidated, but she did acknowledge the message with a sharp nod. Rhonda's earlier quip ran through her mind. *Being around her sexy, single daddy would have some…interesting…advantages.*

Yeah, right.

He was certainly single, and more than sexy, but she doubted those gray eyes would turn smoky and his voice husky because of her. Not that she wanted such a reaction from him, of course, but she suspected this would be one tough assignment from the get-go.

Wade looked at his watch as Myra Jo returned, bearing several brochures. "We need to get going for now. Myra Jo will give you a call. I believe she wants a lunch catered for her sorority friends, so she'll contact you to make arrangements."

With barely time to set an appointment and say their goodbyes, Wade ushered Myra Jo away. Leah stood there, a little dazed, until they disappeared from sight.

Blast it, he'd done it again! With a few words, the man had stolen her composure. That was simply not acceptable. She'd worked for the hard kind before and managed not to get out of sorts. Getting perturbed at this early stage was not a good sign. It would have helped if Wade were old and crotchety, but since that wasn't the case, she'd have to deal sternly with her improper responses to his unfortunate good looks.

Rhonda rejoined her, and the task ahead of them forced Leah to put Wade Mackey from her mind. Except she couldn't quite banish the picture of a rugged, handsome cowboy who looked about as approachable as a bull...right before the gate was pulled.

Wade pulled the gate shut with an irritated jerk and headed for the kitchen, amazed that a week had passed. Sometimes he wondered where all the peace and quiet he tried to guard so fiercely had disappeared to. He warned himself to be careful or he'd land himself in the hospital again with pneumonia.

He wanted to believe he'd learned his lesson, but he glanced at the skyline and shook his head. The sun hadn't even made its appearance and he was already at work. He'd arrived home late last night to have Myra Jo tell him the hot tub wasn't working and her sorority party was the next day—in a few hours, in fact—and Wade had had a hard time teasing her out of her the-world-is-going-to-end mood.

He went into the kitchen and leaned back against the cool ceramic counter, every tile of which had been laid and grouted with his own two hands. He folded his arms across his chest and tried to ignore the coffeepot gurgling behind him, tempting him to check. As usual, his patience ran out before the water in the reservoir, and he poured a mug while drops danced and scuttled on the hot plate. After returning the decanter, he headed back out the door into the predawn coolness.

He'd had to leave from the bridal fair and head directly to the airport to catch his flight to Midland-Odessa. His meeting had gone well with the man who owned the black Angus bull Wade had his sights on, but he was perturbed by the frequency with which his thoughts had been interrupted by the memory of one Leah Houston. In the end, he'd left without the bull because it seemed a stupid time to start indulging his whim for a purebred herd.

Wade paused, taking a careful sip of the strong, hot brew as he watched the gradual lightening of the sky above the scrub-covered hills. There was something amusing about the demarcation between his manicured lawn and the beginnings of the rough soil and tenacious plants of the Texas hill country. Without constant attention, the fragile yard would quickly be taken over by the tough range grasses that defied the rocky soil.

Much like he felt his life was being taken over, at times.

So when had his baby girl grown up? Hadn't he been a band booster and Future Farmers of America sponsor just yesterday? He clearly remembered sitting at the kitchen table, poring over course catalogs with her, back in the days when his opinion had mattered.

What had happened to the giggling girl who could rein

a horse with one hand and hold a portable phone with the other? Somehow she had turned into a beautiful, stubborn woman who wouldn't listen to her daddy when he told her she was picking the wrong man to marry.

Which reminded him—just how had he convinced himself that his attraction to Leah at Tammy's wedding had merely been a healthy man's reaction to a beautiful woman? He'd only attended out of obligation to Tammy, who had been one of Myra Jo's best friends since they were gangly little girls.

But he'd been delighted by the diversion Leah had provided. She'd been cool, contained, an economy of motion, and he'd had the absurd desire to ruffle her feathers, to put a chink in the perfect armor she'd worn around herself. His reaction had surprised him. In fact, he still wondered what it was about her that intrigued him so.

The easy answer was that he was darn near celibate these days. He hardly saw Ysabel anymore, not with the travel demands her new promotion put on her. Even so, his relationship with Ysabel had always been more of a deep, abiding friendship with a little sex thrown in—hardly the typical dating couple, he was sure. So was he drawn to Leah because his body longed to be with a soft, sensual woman, or because he was drawn to her calm, professional demeanor in the midst of all the wedding hysteria? Since he liked to think of himself as being mature enough to handle his sex drive, he wanted to believe the latter.

Yeah, right.

And maybe her lush figure had stood out among the line of nearly anorexic sticks in attendance like a rose in full bloom in a vase full of cattails.

Much more likely.

Seeing Leah and Myra Jo together had also reinforced his concern for his daughter. She was dangerously thin. Not that her mother was any help. The rare times Myra Jo saw Julie, the first words out of Julie's mouth contained a question about whether Myra Jo had gained weight or not. He'd forced himself to stay quiet and wait until after the witch was gone to reassure his baby girl of her intelligence and her beauty. Just thinking about his ex-wife was enough to make his neck ache.

Wade took one last swallow of coffee and threw the dregs from his cup onto the lawn. If he didn't get busy, Leah would be arriving with her crew to find the pool area a mess and the hot tub still not working. He ignored the funny trip of his pulse at the thought of seeing her again. After all, hadn't he just convinced himself that there was nothing unusual about his reaction to the curvy brunette?

As he worked on the pump in its crowded little shed, he reminded himself with each twist of the wrench that he'd better get his libido under control. He might have allowed himself a small fantasy or two at the Griffen wedding, but Leah worked for him now, and he wasn't about to let any nonsense happen.

"Excuse me..." a hesitant voice said from the doorway.

He knew who owned the voice, even though the bright sun backlit Leah's form and hid her face in shadows. Her full curves cast an intriguing picture, and he was stunned as the desire to find out what her softness would feel like if pressed between him and, say, the nearest wall ripped through him.

He pulled himself up short, amazed by the suddenness and intensity of his reaction. Hadn't he just told himself to get his thoughts under control?

At the rate things were going, this wedding would be the death of him.

Two

"Excuse me," Leah repeated, peering into the dim room. "Do you work here?"

She groaned when the man stood up and her eyes adjusted from the brilliant sunshine. She felt like a fool for asking Wade Mackey if he worked there, but he was supposed to be out of town.

"I'm sorry, Wade, I didn't—"

"Don't worry about it." He stepped outside the pump house with her and retrieved his shirt. "Much to Myra Jo's disappointment, I try hard not to look the part of the landed gentry."

Now there was the unvarnished truth. If there was one thing Wade Mackey looked like, it was a dyed-in-the-wool cowboy. Make that Cowboy, with a capital *C,* she amended as she watched him slip the blue chambray shirt over his muscular arms and broad chest. Her mouth went dry as she watched his long fingers work the buttons, slowly hiding the enticing view from her.

"I take it you're ready to set up for the wingding."

Leah nodded, then cleared her throat before adding, "I'm sorry I disturbed you."

"No bother at all. I was getting the hot tub running before Myra Jo calls in the National Guard to contain the disaster."

She tried not to chuckle, but she couldn't help it. "So is it safe to stand down from red alert?"

"Yeah, I think so. I was just about to fire things up and make sure. Did you need my help?"

"Oh, no, I just wanted to be sure it was all right for me to get started. We've got a lot to do before the girls arrive."

"Help yourself to anything you need. I can call some of the boys up from the bunkhouse if you'd like."

"Heavens, no, but thanks for the offer. I wouldn't dream of taking the men away from their duties."

"Their duties are to do whatever I tell them to do."

Leah focused sharply on his words. In a second's span, the good ol' boy had been replaced by the boss. And she strongly doubted the warning she'd heard had been her imagination.

"Be that as it may, I have things under control," she said in a polite tone. There was always some jockeying for position at the start of any job, and Leah had to be careful to establish her inability to be intimidated. Her fleeting hope that Wade's tenseness at the convention center had been a momentary thing faded as fast as the dew under the sweltering Texas sun.

"Then I'll leave you to your work. By the way," he said over his shoulder as he headed back to his repairs, "get with me before you leave. We need to talk without Myra Jo around."

"Fine. I'll see you early this afternoon and we can visit."

Leah walked toward the house to start her crew at their tasks, replaying the last few moments in her head. There

was no doubt she had just been ordered—politely, of
course—to be available to receive her instructions. Leah
had never dreamed she would be working exclusively with
Myra Jo. Since the girl's mother was living in Dallas, it
was easy to extrapolate Daddy Wade would be the PIC,
otherwise known as the parent in charge.

Leah found that during the course of the morning she
could hardly keep her mind off her coming meeting with
him. She directed the luncheon on autopilot, and, thank
goodness, everything went off flawlessly. But by the time
the last cup of coffee had been served, and Myra Jo and
her sorority sisters were lounging by the pool, Leah's
nerves were stretched thin.

With a trepidation she rarely felt, she went to the house
to find Wade. The only person she found inside was a
young woman who spoke little English. Leah caught *uno
momento, por favor* and then *Señor Mackey.* The girl
pointed down the hall so Leah smiled and said, "Gracias,"
then headed in that direction.

Instead of finding Wade's office, however, she walked
straight into his bedroom. The decor was unabashedly masculine. From the cream-and-blue curtains to the massive
wooden furniture, it emanated strength. The faint smell of
toothpaste and aftershave hung in the air. She felt like a
fool for blushing as she stared at the rumpled sheets and
comforter on the king-size bed, only to have her uneasiness
increase when the image of him standing at the sink, shaving, filled her mind.

She quickly returned to the center of the house, ill at
ease with her unintentional snooping, to find an office also
carrying Wade's unmistakable stamp. Although the smell
of leather and rich mahogany furniture weren't uniquely
male, in this case she had little doubt who usually sat behind the large desk, his dark head bent over papers stacked
in seemingly haphazard piles.

Her inspection was interrupted by the excited yips of a beautiful border collie. The dog came into the office and danced around Leah's legs on dainty feet. Leah couldn't help but grin.

"Some guard dog you are!" she scolded. The dog was clearly unimpressed, for her hind end only wagged harder as Leah read the metal tag shaped like the state of Texas attached to the collar.

"Where's the boss man, Spoiled Rotten? Where's Daddy?"

Rotten's black-tipped ears perked up, and she raced around the desk to jump into the chair.

"I know this is his office, silly."

But the collie merely circled in the chair and barked.

"All right, all right." Refusing to believe she was conversing with a dog, Leah sat on one of the two matching wingbacks facing the large desk. After five minutes, she thought about finding the maid again, but decided that would be futile. After five more minutes of crossing and uncrossing her legs, she finally gave Wade's stand-in a glare.

"Look, he may be the boss, but that doesn't give him the right to keep me cooling my heels."

Rotten just wagged her tail.

With a frustrated sigh, she wrote Wade a note and tore the page from her day planner. She included a business card before placing them in a relatively clear space on his blotter. With a final pat on Rotten's silky head, she went home.

Her drive was uneventful, but as she neared Austin, Leah began to regret leaving without finding Wade. She couldn't afford to mess up this opportunity to redeem her reputation, but at the same time, she wasn't a servant at Wade's beck and call. She had things to do, and waiting on an autocratic cowboy wasn't one of them—even if that stubborn cowboy held her career in his hands.

The phone was ringing when she unlocked the door to her office. She glanced at her neat, black-lacquer desk and her floral print couch and armchairs. Elegantly draped white tiebacks muted the bright sunshine, creating an exquisite decor. Oddly, she couldn't stop the image of dark wood and stacked papers from flashing across her mind.

She almost didn't answer the persistent ringing—she had planned to use this rare weekend with no events scheduled to catch up on her paperwork, but her conscience prevailed.

"Leah Houston."

"I thought I told you I wanted to talk with you."

So much for chitchat.

"You did, and I tried to find you. When I couldn't, I left a note on your desk."

"I know, I smelled your perfume."

Leah couldn't stop the thrill that ran up her spine.

"I was in the barn," he continued. "Someone should have told you."

"The only person I found was your maid, and we had a little trouble communicating."

"That would be Amalia, my foreman's daughter. We're working on her English since she wants to go to college next year." He paused. "We have a ways to go."

She was surprised by the dryly affectionate tone in his voice. He already had a habit of doing that…surprising her. She didn't like it.

"Yes, well, my Spanish is exceptionally rusty, and I'm not psychic, so I apologize for missing you." Feeling a little silly, she crossed her fingers before saying, "I can come back later this afternoon, if you'd like."

"No, I'd rather meet without Myra Jo around, and her friends have left."

She released a silent breath and uncrossed her fingers.

"How about dinner this evening instead?"

She frowned at the phone. So much for luck….

"I don't—"

"If you'll give me directions to your place, I can pick you up about eight."

Leah took a deep breath and held it. As she slowly exhaled, she reminded herself that she had worked with difficult clients before. Sometimes she had to compromise to get what she wanted. Reluctantly, she gave him instructions to her condo.

Although she tried to work, it soon became clear she wasn't going to get anything accomplished. Her mind wouldn't stay on task. Visions of Wade—his naked chest bathed in the morning sun, a sardonic twist curving his lips—kept appearing before her eyes. Forty-two-year-old men were supposed to have the beginnings of a paunch and receding hairlines. They certainly weren't supposed to look as though they could pose for fitness magazines.

With a frustrated sigh, she repacked her briefcase and headed home.

It wasn't until she was sitting on her bed some hours later, gathering one leg of her panty hose in her fingers and mourning the loss of her lazy evening of air-popped popcorn and channel surfing, that Leah realized how tense she was.

Bra, hose, slip, low-heeled pumps, jewelry—the works—when she could be in old sweats and her favorite holey red socks. She tugged on a rayon coatdress and artfully tucked a silk scarf into the deep neckline. She had no idea what Mr. Mackey had in mind, but this was a dinner meeting, not a dinner date.

She had just clasped her watch around her wrist when the doorbell rang. She checked her appearance in the mirror and smiled wryly at her reflection. He was punctual, she could say that for him.

She opened the door to find her breath taken away once again. Half-naked, he had been nearly indescribable. In creased black jeans, a white dress shirt open at the neck, a sports jacket and boots, Wade was nothing short of yummy. The black Stetson he reached up to remove from his head made him the quintessential cowboy.

And she'd purged cowboys from her fantasy list a long time ago, she reminded herself. She wanted a nineties man, an urbane one, one who treated her as an equal, a partner. Cowboys weren't known for their modern mind-sets.

It took a stern mental rap to get her hand off the knob and welcome him inside. Her fortitude returned when his gaze raked over her dress and she had the distinct impression she'd lost marks on his tally stick.

"Can I get you something to drink?"

"No, thanks. Nice place."

"But not your style," she offered helpfully.

"No, I reckon not."

"Let me grab my purse, then, and we'll get going."

Once outside, she was ready to find a pickup truck waiting. What she hadn't expected was a bright yellow Mustang. She hadn't taken Wade for the sports car type, but maybe she'd misjudged him. Could her perceptions be that far off?

He laughed when he saw her expression. "Not exactly a limousine, I admit. I had to bring my truck into town for some work so I borrowed a friend's car. Or rather, I ended up with my friend's son's car."

Leah blushed. "I'm sorry, I didn't mean to be rude. I was just caught off guard."

His manners were flawless as he helped her into the car, but that was no surprise. Country boy or not, he was a gentleman. And she wasn't surprised when he pulled into the crowded parking lot at the Broken Spoke. She'd hardly expected him to take her to the country club, considering the man she was coming to know, and she had no doubt she was being tested again. Well, she'd eaten her share of chicken-fried steak, and she could probably remember how to dance the schottische in a pinch.

As soon as the waitress had taken their orders, Leah got down to business. "What would you like to talk about first?"

Wade folded his hands on the table in front of him. "I don't like Pennington Bradford, and I don't like his daddy even more. But I do love my daughter, and I want her to be happy."

He paused. Leah waited.

"Myra Jo doesn't think so, but I was young once, and I remember what it was like to be impulsive, to believe love was enough to solve any problem. I don't think she has a clue what she's facing if she goes through with this marriage, and I'd do anything to keep her from getting hurt."

Warning bells went off in Leah's head. "I think most fathers feel as you do," she said, treading softly.

He raised one eyebrow. "Even in this day and age, I don't think *most* fathers raise their daughters by themselves."

Despite her earlier vow to be cautious, Leah decided to go ahead and say what was on her mind. If Wade was as up-front as he claimed, he'd respect her. If he wasn't, it would be better to lose the contract now instead of risking a second disaster.

"Wade, I've been doing this for a long time, and one thing I'm sure of is that it's a mistake to play God. I've seen couples I was certain were doomed become inseparable, and vice versa. So if you're asking me to help you to keep Myra Jo from marrying Pennington, I'm afraid I can't oblige you."

Wade cast her an amused glance. "I'm not asking you to. I know the quickest way to get a child to do something is to forbid it, so my goal hasn't been to stop her. I've dragged things out as long as I could to see if she'd open her eyes.''

"Start seeing things your way, you mean," she said, unable to stop herself.

His look turned mocking. "No, I meant it the way I said it. If I thought she had any inkling of what marrying Pennington really means, I'd feel more at ease. The way it stands, I'm not convinced. The long and short of it is, I'm going to give Myra Jo the biggest wedding money can buy. And I'm also going to do my best to ensure her a chance at a happy future.''

"And if things don't work out that way?" Leah asked quietly.

"Then my little girl can come home, and her daddy'll do his damnedest to heal her broken heart.''

Hot tears sprang into Leah's eyes despite her most valiant effort to contain them. It was clear that Wade would gladly play the bad guy, even risk his daughter's rejection, to assure her happiness. Considering her "I'll do it on my own" philosophy, Leah should have been scornful, convinced Myra Jo would never stand on her own two feet as long as she knew she had her daddy to fall back on. Instead, all she felt was a pang of envy.

"Maybe someday Myra Jo will know how lucky she is to have you for a father," she finally managed to say.

"Maybe," Wade echoed in a lighter tone, "but I'm still not wearing a tuxedo.''

Leah had to roll her eyes, but was grateful that Wade had lightened the mood.

"Come on, Wade. Surely that's just another delaying tactic?''

"Maybe.''

Hope quickened in her breast only to fade as she realized he was serious about not wearing a tuxedo. The wedding was only a month away; now was not the time for him to be unreasonable.

"I'm no weekend cowboy, Leah, living in Westlake and thinking I'm a rancher because I own a few acres and run a few head. I work my land and my herds. My hands get dirty and my boots aren't for show."

He took a breath and continued. "I can still remember the year we got indoor plumbing. I remember the year we didn't eat meat until fall and we butchered a hog. I remember skipping school because I had to help my dad. Those things mold a man."

He studied his clean, square nails.

"My Daddy's word has always been worth more than gold, so if my family wasn't good enough for people like the Bradfords then, we're sure the hell not good enough now."

"I can understand how you feel, but in the end this is your only child's wedding."

"I've told you that I'll give Myra Jo the full three-ring circus, but I won't play the trained bear for anybody."

Wade suddenly looked weary, and Leah felt her heart pull. She had to believe growing up poor was not the only reason Wade was so firmly set in his ways. She wondered if Myra Jo's mother was to blame for him putting up such high walls, or if some other woman had turned him so self-contained.

Whatever the reason—sheer cussedness or deep conviction—it was clear a battle would wage to put some shine on a man who wore his humble beginnings like a badge of honor.

"So," he said, drawing her attention again, "have I scared you off?"

Leah loved a challenge, but she doubted Wade knew how reasonable it was for her to be afraid. Her reputation was at stake. Wade might not think she understood pride, but she did. Just like him, she knew the desire to be judged for who she was, not what she could do or how much money she made. Oh, how she knew the desire for people to see past the trappings and accept her for the woman she was on the inside.

She gave her head a little shake to stop her wandering thoughts. She could take comfort in the fact that Wade would play fair. Tough, but fair. That she could handle.

"Nope," she finally said, holding out her hand. "You may have met your match, Wade Mackey."

He paused a long moment before a smile slowly grew and he took her offered palm. "That would be a rare treat, Leah Houston."

They sat back and let the waitress serve their dinners, and Leah discovered her appetite had returned.

"So what's the next shindig on the list?" Wade asked between bites of steak.

"Myra Jo wants a barbecue as a combination graduation party and official announcement."

"That's right, I'd forgotten. I still think it's pretty silly to 'announce' a year-old engagement."

"I've seen the guest list," Leah said carefully. "It's going to be quite an affair."

His lips tightened. "Bradford's up for reelection and I guess he saw an opportunity to slap backs at my expense. But hell, I don't care."

Leah wasn't sure that was entirely true, but she was sure this wasn't a financial issue. She'd already been given the okay to hire the best caterers in Texas and one of the hottest up-and-coming bands. The decorations alone were no small cost, but the agreement she'd sent him had come back to her desk without a mark on it except his bold signature on the approval line.

"At least attire won't be a fight," she said, trying for some levity. "Denim will be de rigueur."

"You think so?" he said, lifting an eyebrow. "We've already had three fights that my brand of denim isn't good enough. Myra Jo wants to buy me some highfalutin designer jeans and have boots custom-made for the occasion. My Tony Lama's will be just fine with a little spit and polish."

Since they were back to square one, Leah decided to let things go for now. She only had a week until the barbecue, but then she would have another two until the rehearsal. Surely she could find a way to make him change his mind in three weeks. After all, she'd gotten the governor to dress up as The Beast so his daughter could be Belle at a costume party, hadn't she?

The conversation drifted into the mundane for the rest of the meal, and the evening took on a delightful air. It wasn't until the check arrived that they once again squared off.

Wade reached for it at the same time she did. His face took on that stubborn expression Leah decided she'd better get used to, so she finally let go. The test of wills had only taken a matter of seconds, but the battle had been real.

How foolish of her even to think of picking up the tab, even though the meal was a business deduction for her. He might only be seven years her senior, but feminism seemed to have passed this cowboy by without even ruffling his hair.

Leah noted Wade's generous tip with absurd pleasure. She might have scratched cowboys off her fantasy list, but selfish men had never even been a consideration.

"Look, Leah, I've had about all the arguing I can stand. I clean up real good, so I can promise you I won't show up at the barbecue, or even the wedding, in overalls. You just take care of Myra Jo and don't worry about me."

Oh, sure. That should be a breeze. Just as it had been a breeze to reserve the country club for the reception on such short notice, and book the caterer who was usually scheduled a year in advance, and cajole the baker into guaranteeing a five-tiered bride's cake, a groom's cake and the numerous extras required for an affair this size. What had Myra Jo been thinking to send out her invitations without these details planned? Now she could add getting the world's most stubborn cowboy into a cutaway.

Any more "easy" tasks and she might just scream.

She calmed her wayward thoughts as Wade led her to the car, keeping a solicitous hand on her elbow. The evening sky was filled with a billion twinkling diamonds, and the quiet wrapped around them, incongruously making the parking lot seem intimate after the music-filled evening.

She wasn't expecting the thrill that raced through her veins when he stopped and turned to give her an inscrutable look.

"Would you like to go for a walk on Town Lake before I take you home?"

Years of practice allowed Leah to keep her astonishment hidden. No, their meeting hadn't been a date by the usual definition, but she probed her memory and found many real dates which hadn't been this enjoyable.

Why did she find Wade's interest in her companionship so hard to believe? Why was she looking for ulterior motives when the man might simply wish to spend some time with her? They'd had a pleasant evening, and all he wanted was to go for a walk by the lake.

Perhaps most surprising of all, she wanted to accept the impromptu invitation.

"That sounds lovely."

The short drive down Lamar Boulevard was companionable. Leah congratulated herself on being able to put Wade a bit more at ease, and hoped she was building a good foundation to work from when things got dicey. For now, she decided to follow Wade's example and enjoy the moment.

She matched his slow pace as they strolled along the Town Lake trail. The moon, pregnant with summer promise, reflected off the Colorado River. Pecan and cypress trees held hands over their heads, flirting with the night wind.

The occasional lap of the water against the bank, the crunch of gravel under the wheels of a passing bicycle, and the muted sound of traffic from the street only made the solitude seem safer, more comfortable. When they reached the rock overlook departing from the trail, it seemed entirely natural to lean her arms on the railing beside Wade's and watch the lights from the power plant dance on the water. If it were earlier in the day, they'd be visited by the ducks and swans in search of a handout, but they had all found their nests, leaving the humans to enjoy the evening in relative peace and quiet.

Leah shivered when a gust of wind chased down her spine.

"Are you cold?" Wade asked, concern coloring his voice.

"No, just goose bumps. I've lived in Texas all my life, so you'd think I'd be used to the scorching hot days and cool nights of early summer in these parts."

"Or maybe a rabbit hopped over your grave."

She tilted her head. "Now there's a pleasant colloquialism!"

Leah looked back out over the water. On the surface, Wade seemed content to stand in companionable silence, but she sensed a controlled hunger in him. It was her business to read people, and her instincts said his confident bearing was hiding something. Maybe she simply recognized a kindred spirit, a soul not yet fulfilled, a yearning for something ineffable.

Those thoughts making her want to reach out to him also awakened the little voice that had served her well over the years. And the voice reminded her to tread carefully. Wade had not invited an intimacy with her, and in fact, the very idea was illogical to contemplate. If anything, Leah knew better than to mix business with…anything else.

"Wade, it's been a nice evening and all—"

"But…"

"But I've had a long day and my nap is wearing off."

One side of his mouth tipped upward. "That's an awfully roundabout way of saying you want to go home."

"In my business, you learn subtlety."

"Meaning you have to fib to get what you want?"

"Not fibbing, exactly. More like…redirecting."

"So instead of telling the groom's mother she looks like a purple sausage in the outfit she's wearing, you'd do what? Give her a gift certificate to a dress shop?"

Leah was losing the fight against a grin. "I'd probably mention to her how lovely she'd look in peach, with her hair and complexion, and ask her if she'd seen the new collection by a designer I think would flatter her."

"Very good!" Wade took his hat off and set it on the flat rocks off to his right. "So if I told you I wanted to haul you into my arms and kiss the daylights out of you, you'd say…?"

Leah's jaw worked silently for a second or two before she realized she probably looked like a fish out of water. Heaven knew she shouldn't be this flustered, but he'd managed to blindside her yet again.

She cleared her throat and said, "I'd probably say…um…something like I was flattered but it wouldn't be a good idea. Yes! I'd tell you it would be foolish for you to kiss me since I'm going to be working so closely with you and your family and…uh…kissing, as it were, would be inappropriate since—"

Her words were cut off as his mouth closed over hers, a warm, firm pressure that served effectively to silence her.

As he pulled her into the steely strength of his arms, she was forced to wonder again if she were dreaming. She felt the wind snatch away the scarf Wade had dislodged, the slide of silk against her sensitized skin almost harsh.

She tried to think, tried to concentrate. She never lost control. Ever. And she wanted to deny her will was being drained so easily. Not her, no-nonsense Leah, who never wasted time in hopeless moments of pure whimsy. She simply couldn't be standing on the Town Lake trail kissing a man she barely knew.

Surely it wasn't she, melted against a rugged cowboy's length, feeling the cool smoothness of his buttons slide provocatively against her breast...feeling the hardness of his sex pressed intimately at the apex of her thighs and the gentle scratch of his callused thumb against her throat, sending tremors down her spine.

Leah gasped softly as his kiss deepened and his hands moved against the fabric of her dress, pulling her just the slightest bit closer. Her awareness of him increased, if that were possible, making his chest feel like a granite wall against her softness, making her fingers clutch the bulging muscles of his biceps, making her swear she'd have a denim pattern stamped on her thighs for a week after this.

Oh, but it would be worth it. She felt vibrantly alive and thoroughly desired, feelings she couldn't ever remember feeling.

With a shuddering breath Wade abruptly set her away from him and turned back to the railing, clenching the cool metal so tightly his knuckles showed white.

"Leah, I apologize. I've never been quite so...impulsive...before."

Impulsive? She was still standing there like a dazed idiot and he was worrying about being impulsive?

Somehow she forced a brain cell to work and stepped back one more pace. With an unexpectedly even tone, she said, "Please don't apologize. You've only proven my point. We need to maintain a proper relationship if we're going to work together to make Myra Jo's wedding a success."

Wade pushed off the rail and picked up his hat. He seemed inordinately preoccupied with brushing away non-existent particles of dust. "That might be good."

He straightened then and walked a few steps down the trail to retrieve her scarf. His eyes seemed drawn against his will to the skin exposed by the vee of her dress, but he forced himself to look away. A shiver that had nothing to do with the breeze shook her. His gaze had flowed over her like warm, gray smoke, and combined with his citrusy aftershave still in her nostrils, it was overwhelming to her still-dazed senses.

She accepted his offered arm, and they walked to the car as if nothing had happened, but she was glad he couldn't see the hand holding the strip of silk. The fabric would never be the same from being clenched in her fist.

During the ride to her house, Wade was as congenial as a woman could hope a man to be. And she amazed herself by responding in a normal voice.

"I'd like you to come out and meet my folks," Wade said as he took the turn into her neighborhood. "If you think Myra Jo wants you to groom me a bit—"

"She didn't say—"

"Leah," he said shortly, "I'm nobody's fool."

This was not new information to her. "Certainly. I can come out anytime," she said as they reached her condo and Wade walked her to her door.

"Well," she said a shade brightly, all too aware of the dreaded end of the evening. "Would you like to come in for a nightcap or cup of coffee?"

"No, thank you. I'll be headed back to the homestead. Do you think you could come out tomorrow and meet my folks?"

Tomorrow was Sunday, and for once her calendar was free. Spring and summer months usually had her at some church or hall every weekend, but her new executive assistant was taking the Baker affair, leaving Leah the illusion of having one whole day to laze around the condo.

"Don't you think I should call first and set an appointment?"

"Heck no! You go all stiff and formal on my dad and he'll be a pain in the——" Wade cleared his throat quickly. "I mean, he'll be difficult to deal with. Myra Jo's terrified of what her grandfather's going to pull in a roomful of politicians and their cronies."

"It's a wonder she doesn't elope," Leah muttered under her breath.

"And please don't come all citified," Wade warned, ignoring her comment, if he'd even heard it. "Take your hair out of that knot and put on a pair of jeans, for God's sake."

A short laugh burst from her lips. "Yes, sir."

Wade looked annoyed, but Leah wanted to believe the distracted look meant he was upset with himself, not her.

"I apologize," he said. "It's just nearly driven me crazy all evening to see that beautiful hair of yours all mashed back. I've been imagining it would look like liquid chocolate and feel like silk. It's been all I could do to keep my hands off."

Her face flushed hotly. She always wore her hair up, unless she was at home or in an extremely casual situation. Without thinking, she put a self-conscious hand to her ear.

"I'll do my best tomorrow."

"Good. I'll see you then." Leaning forward, he placed a kiss on her cheek. "Good night, Leah."

She had the foolish urge to turn her face so their lips would meet.

"Good night, Wade."

As she closed the door behind her, the silence of her professionally cleaned and decorated apartment surrounded her. She walked into the dimly lit living room and glanced around. For some silly reason, all she could think of was Wade going home to his daughter and the excited greeting of a beautiful collie. She, on the other hand, would say good-night to an expensive painting and curl up in bed with the printout her accountant had dropped by yesterday.

Yep, she decided as she headed for her bedroom, she had it all.

Wade settled into a comfortable cruising speed, noting absently that Highway 290 wasn't crowded this time of night. It was too late for commuting traffic and too early for the drunks headed home. But Wade's mind was bumper-to-bumper with jumbled thoughts.

He couldn't figure out what was wrong with him. He didn't think he'd ever acted so irrationally with a woman before. The need to kiss her had just overwhelmed him, and he'd been helpless to resist the urge to pull her into his arms.

He called himself a thousand kinds of fool. And the foolishness had to stop. There was too much at stake for him to be acting irresponsibly. His daughter's happiness was more important than his hormones.

But he couldn't deny that that not-so-simple kiss had been a soul-rocking event, something of a shock to a man who thought spontaneous combustion was mere theory. Lord help him if he had been in a position to go any further. He doubted he would have come to his senses until he'd buried himself inside her and found release.

He'd meant what he'd said. He was never impulsive. Yet

even now, while worrying that his daughter was giving him the fastest-forming ulcer in history, his mind would not let go of the image of making Leah lose control with him, driving her mindless with passion underneath him. She was so contained, so self-assured, he wanted to rock her as deeply as she'd rocked him. He wanted her primal...not sleek and oh-so-correct.

He shook his head sharply. Yes, he was attracted to Leah, but he'd just met her, for criminy's sake. Of course, she'd thrown him off guard by not reacting to his ''I'm the boss'' speech as he'd expected, and there was nothing like surprise to intrigue a man. He'd been so sure she would disapprove of his motives. Not that approval or disapproval mattered, but she had empathized with him, and for the first time in months he felt a little less like bubblegum stuck to the bottom of a shoe.

Oh, he'd definitely seen the wheels beginning to turn in her beautiful head when the discussion had inevitably turned to the damned tuxedo issue, but he was sure he could hold his own with her. No amount of coaxing from Myra Jo had changed his mind, so he doubted the machinations of the curvaceous consultant would have any better effect.

He was sure of one thing, though—

The sound of a siren and bright strobe lights in his rearview mirror jerked him rudely to attention.

Without hesitation he pulled onto the shoulder and cut his engine while he rolled down the window. He was reaching for his wallet when he heard a vaguely familiar voice.

''All right, Bobby Ray, I clocked you at ninety-two. I've caught your—oh! Mr. Mackey!''

''Evenin', Tim.''

Wade looked out the window at a boy he'd almost raised. Tim Anderson's folks were some of his best friends, and Tim and Myra Jo had gone to school together since grade school. Then Myra Jo had gone off to college and Tim had gone to the Department of Public Safety academy. Wade had even attended the boy's graduation.

"What are you doing in Bobby Ray's Mustang, Mr. Mackey?"

Wade got out of the car and leaned back against the quarter panel. He rubbed the tension lines on his forehead. "It's a long story, Tim."

"Well, uh, did you know how fast you were going?"

"No, Tim, I'm afraid I didn't. I was daydreaming a bit."

"That's dangerous at any speed, Mr. Mackey, but certainly at over ninety."

"I know, son."

"Well, if you'll give me your word you'll watch it the rest of the way home, I'll let you go."

"I appreciate it."

Wade held his hand out to the young man, remembering the time when Tim had solemnly informed him that men didn't hug. If he recalled correctly, Tim had been about seven.

He'd almost slid back into his seat when a thought occurred to him. Stepping back out, he called to Tim. "How'd you know this was Bobby Ray's car?"

Tim's laugh carried the few feet between the vehicles. "Bobby Ray and I used to drag out here in high school. I told him when I became a Trooper I was going to nail his butt someday. I thought I had my chance tonight."

"Sorry to disappoint you, son."

"No problem. You just slow down and drive more like a man your age should. You got that?"

Wade chuckled. "Yeah, I got it. And you're gonna get it, too, as soon as I catch you out of uniform."

"Now, Mr. Mackey, don't make me haul you in for threatening an officer."

"You know me, Tim. I don't threaten. I promise."

Tim laughed again as he slipped inside his vehicle and

turned off his strobes. Wade indulged in another chuckle as he pulled back onto the highway, determined to set aside his obsession with one particular lady. No matter how beautiful she was, he wasn't going to get a ticket. Or worse.

"Drive like a man my age, my foot!" Wade snorted. "That pup thinks anyone over thirty is old, but I've got news for him."

He might have edged past forty, but he was hardly over the hill. He had a long life ahead of him.

His smile faded. Long and alone, if the truth were told. Myra Jo was starting her new life, and he felt as if his had gone into limbo.

He used to know exactly who he was and what he had to do. He was a single father, a son and a rancher. He used to get up every day before the sun, knowing he had a family to support and more bills to pay than money to pay them with. Now his baby was leaving, he was starting to parent his parents and he had people running the ranch for him. He was supposed to be free to do the things he wanted, but running the ranch *was* what he wanted.

Did this mean he was in a midlife crisis? He'd always thought the midlife crisis thing was a bunch of hogwash people used to excuse their misbehavior.

Hell, he decided he wasn't sure about anything anymore.

Except his inability to get his mind off one beautiful, elegant brunette.

Three

Leah checked her hair self-consciously before she left the sanctuary of her car. She'd spent the entire drive to Wade's vacillating between congratulating herself on her casual attire and berating herself for obeying him. She'd picked her oldest and most faded pair of pleated jeans and had added a simple cotton top knotted over a peach-colored tank. Her only wish was that jeans did a better job of masking the few extra pounds giving her hips a roundness not exactly in style these days. She hadn't cared what a man thought about her body in a long time, and it made her uncomfortable to acknowledge that she wanted Wade to think she was attractive.

During the time her mind wasn't occupied with those thoughts, she had lectured herself not to make a fool of herself when she saw him again. She absolutely forbade her heart to flutter, her stomach to constrict and her pulse to race. He was just a man, for heaven's sake, and the father of her client. The man who, incidentally, would be writing her a check.

The man who'd kissed her as though her lips tasted of honey.

The man whose touch had reminded her how very long it had been since she'd felt desired.

With a fortifying breath she gathered her purse and planner and headed toward the house. As she expected, Wade answered the doorbell. Unexpectedly, though, she went a little light-headed—in spite of her self-directed lectures.

But it was his fault, she decided. No available forty-something man should be this good-looking. If he were married or attached it would make sense for him to be this handsome. The ones that were taken always were. The available ones—at least the ones she'd met—usually seemed a little desperate.

She found she wasn't attracted to desperate men. Go figure....

"Good morning," he said, taking in her boots, jeans and French-braided hair. His short nod of approval irked her, and she was glad for the uncomfortable feeling. It kept her from reading too much into the little smile that curved his lips and lifted the corners of his eyes.

"You look beautiful."

It wasn't fair. Even his voice was gorgeous. How was she supposed to stay irritated if he wouldn't cooperate?

"Thank you." She determinedly made her voice light, and ignored the pleasant tingle his compliment gave her. "I hope I'm not too early."

"Not at all. It's refreshing to have a woman show up when she says she will." Wade squinted one eye shut. "Oops, I probably shouldn't have said that."

Leah gave him a lopsided smile as she shook her head. "Wade, you may not be politically correct, but you're probably the most straightforward man I've ever met."

He tipped his head to the left. "And that's a good thing?"

"Yes, it is."

He gave an exaggerated sigh of relief. "Well, thank the Lord for small blessings."

"Are your folks ready to meet me?" she asked as she followed him to the kitchen, trying to gain some equilibrium. He was so stern one minute and smiling the next. She wondered if he was doing it on purpose—just to keep her flustered.

"Myra Jo and my brother, Jonathan, went to church with them, and we're supposed to meet at Mama's for lunch. I hope you haven't eaten."

"Not since breakfast, but I really don't want to intrude on your parents—"

"Trust me. Mama is in her glory when she's feeding people. You'll win her over forever if you praise her cooking."

"If you say so."

"And I have to warn you. If you think I'm a straight shooter, there's no telling what my daddy might pop off with. Your best defense is to not act shocked."

"I'll keep that in mind." Leah wondered, not for the first time, just what she'd gotten herself into.

"Great. Since we've got some time, why don't I show you around the place a bit? Then we'll head down the road."

Curiosity more than politeness made her agree. The blandness of his expression should have told her he had something up his sleeve, but it wasn't until they went out the back door that the sight of two saddled horses made her realize what it was.

She stopped in her tracks and gave him a sardonic glance.

"I don't suppose you have a Jeep we could use instead?'' She tried to disguise the near terror building in her stomach.

Wade turned from checking the cinch on a saddle. She assumed the reddish brown horse was for her since it was smaller than the black behemoth that looked as if he wanted to take a bite out of her.

''Are you going to tell me you've lived in Texas all your life and you've never been on a horse?''

She gave an exasperated snort. ''Wade, lots of people in Texas have never been on a horse.''

''Not true natives.''

She knew he was teasing her, but she still felt a little defensive. ''Yes, even true natives.''

''You're not scared, are you?''

Leah rarely felt inclined to answer taunts, as she rarely cared what people thought about her personally. Professionally yes. Otherwise they could take her or leave her.

But for some strange reason, she found she cared very much what Wade thought of her. And even more surprising, she had to admit the wedding had nothing to do with it. She wanted Wade to like *her,* not just respect her as a businesswoman.

That interesting thought deserved more attention, so she filed it away for later inspection.

''No, I'm not scared.''

He raised an eyebrow.

''I'm terrified.''

He raised the other, but his expression contained a generous dose of sympathy.

''But,'' she said, taking a solid breath and continuing, ''I'm willing to try this if you'll be patient with me.''

Besides, she rationalized, her efforts might pay off when it came time for the next round on the tuxedo issue.

''Deal.'' He studied her for a moment and then said, ''Wait here. I'll be right back.''

As he went into the house, Leah watched the horses warily and muttered, "And where would I go?"

The black brute snuffled and shifted his hooves, making Leah jump back, her heart racing. She knew nothing about horses and here she was baby-sit—er...horse-sitting as if she would know what to do if one of the two beasts decided to run away.

Wade returned before she could talk herself out of the whole deal. When he handed her a beautifully shaped cowboy hat, she let out a sigh.

"Great, Wade. First you want to scare me to death, then you want to give me hat hair. Thanks a lot."

He simply smiled and put the tan felt on her head. "It's one of Myra Jo's. I figured you two'd be close in size."

The hat was a bit small, but not uncomfortably so. Leah decided it was prudent to keep playing Wade's game at this point. She sent a mental fax to the fairness gods to make sure she was earning points for this.

Leah nearly fainted when he introduced her to the monster named Thunder and then to Thumper. The little mare stretched her nose closer, and Wade had the poor grace to laugh at her stricken expression.

"She wants you to blow back in her nose, Leah."

"You're kidding, right?"

"Nope. Watch."

She was fascinated to see the horse brighten from his attention. Wade finally convinced her to try it, but only laughed at her again.

"That wasn't a blow. That wasn't even a sneeze. Come on, Leah, this animal weighs seven times as much as you do. Blow!"

When she did, she earned another snuffle from Thumper and actually felt her fear lighten a small notch.

Finally Wade gave her a quick course in mounting before helping her onto Thumper with surprisingly little discomfort on her part, considering his proximity. His face near her thighs and his hands on her calves as he adjusted her stirrups might have caused her blood to heat and her face to flush, but it wasn't from embarrassment.

She admitted feeling envy as she watched him take his seat on Thunder's muscular back. His fluid grace as he mounted told her he'd done this countless times, and it was as natural to him as breathing. She may not have been on a horse herself, but being a "true native," she could deduce a real horseman.

Suddenly Thunder didn't seem so frightening with Wade sitting confidently, almost negligently, in the saddle. She didn't care how corny it sounded, he looked as if he'd been born there. And it was easy to see how the mystique of a cowboy had lured more than one feminine heart down the garden path.

Which she would do well to remember.

Instead her imagination rolled right over the warning. Wade carried the essence of a born-and-bred Texan male, something that couldn't be purchased at a Western-wear store. All the boots leather could make would never endow the wearer with the long-limbed stride so much a part of Wade Mackey. Leah had little doubt he also held the code-of-the-West attitude that tended to make the feminist in her twitch; but at the same time, she felt a traitorous thrill when she wondered what it would be like to be loved and protected by this unapologetically alpha male.

Of course, she could never admit such feelings or she might have to forfeit her lifetime subscription to *Cosmopolitan.*

All too soon Wade had them moving, and she was too busy concentrating on staying atop the docile mare to indulge in any more thoughts of Wade. He kept a slow pace, offering advice on how to hold her reins, to relax, to trust her horse and so many other helpful tips she actually started to enjoy the morning.

"Look up, Leah."

When she did, she realized there was more to see than the shiny fur between her horse's ears. Wade had led them to the top of a rise, and the panorama spread out before them was starkly beautiful. The gently rolling hills that gave the area its name marked the horizon, and the land in between was sectioned off in huge chunks by the wooden posts and barbed wire that had changed the course of Texas history a century before.

Cattle grazed in one pasture, and in another, deep green alfalfa stirred in the gentle breeze.

There was obviously much more beyond her line of sight, and Leah had to restrain the urge to turn Thumper around and go exploring. The only thing keeping her from indulging her impulsive thought was the knowledge that she was literally along for the ride. Her horse easily followed Wade's lead and hardly seemed inclined to go off gallivanting by itself.

She was stunned when she glanced at her watch and saw nearly an hour had passed as they'd toured a small bit of Wade's ranch. Other than his occasional tour-guide comments, she'd simply enjoyed the silence and his company. It had been years, if ever, since she remembered being with a man and feeling so utterly comfortable. The thought was as delightful as it was disconcerting.

Her sudden tension must have transmitted itself to Thumper because the mare decided to back up.

"Loosen up on the reins, Leah."

His voice shocked her into doing exactly what he asked, albeit by accident. Thumper settled immediately, and Wade gave her an odd look.

"Are you all right?"

"I'm fine," she fibbed. "Just daydreaming."

Wade nodded. "Me, too."

His tone piqued her curiosity. "Penny for your thoughts."

He smiled. "I think you're offering too much, but I was thinking about a section of my land on the north border. I've got some fence to repair on one of my best grazing areas. One of Senator Bradford's pet road projects would have chopped it up, but I managed to block the bill."

Leah nodded, remembering the story in the paper and how impressed she'd been. A reporter had gotten a damaging, sound bite on Bradford when he'd discovered Wade's success, and the unguarded moment had nearly cost the Senator reelection. It was obvious Wade played hardball when he had to.

That article had led to another in *Texas Monthly*. The full-page close-up in the layout had taken her breath away. She'd read every word describing the Mackey rags-to-riches story, and had thought the journalist mean-spirited to tell the story of how Wade had worn a rented tuxedo to an inaugural ball, commenting under a picture of him standing next to Myra Jo that she didn't seem afflicted by a similar lack of style. Leah had wondered if the author hadn't been a friend of Mr. Bradford's.

The pictures and the article had been the topic of gossip at several weddings she'd done shortly after the issue ran, but Leah had come to believe that Wade Mackey was some of what the article had said, but a whole lot more of what it hadn't. He was fiercely protective of his family and a very private person, traits irresistible to the media. And knowing Wade, she was sure his father had equally despised the article, which revealed he'd had two heart attacks and bypass surgery.

She brought her attention back to Wade. "I imagine you're not the senator's most favorite person, then."

"Hardly. I dread the day he tries to use Myra Jo against

me." Wade's hands tightened on the reins as he turned his horse around. "He won't try anything right away, but I have no doubt he'll try to manipulate my help on some project or another, and then Myra Jo will be in the middle."

Leah could hardly deny his theory when she knew so little about Bradford, but there was no doubting Wade believed the prospect was inevitable.

Leah turned her horse, mimicking his use of reins and clicking her tongue, but with considerably less finesse.

"Are we heading back?" she asked.

"Yes, I took us in an arc from my place to Mama's, so we're not far. I think we've given everyone time to get out of their Sunday best, and they'll be more comfortable."

She shifted in the saddle and thought she saw amusement on Wade's face, but she'd sell snow cones for Satan before admitting her rump was numb.

Wade led her to his parents' house, which would have been a little less than a mile from his home down a long, winding lane. Or an hour on horseback by the scenic route.

"Wait just a second and I'll help you," he said as they came to a stop.

In one of those instant moments of clarity, Leah knew her stubborn pride was about to get her into trouble. Even so, she couldn't stop herself from trying to dismount unassisted.

It was her own fault. She managed to swing down just fine, but hadn't considered how an hour on horseback for the inexperienced tended to make the knees a little shaky the first few moments back on terra firma.

He'd told her to wait for him, but no-o-o-o-o, she had to decide she knew more than the professional horseman. The nightmare started when her legs gave way beneath her. She grabbed for the saddle and ended up—just as she'd dreaded—on her behind, in the dust, at the feet of the most handsome man she'd ever met.

"Leah!" Wade squatted beside her. "Are you hurt?"

She wondered just how red her neck and cheeks were. "Just my feelings."

He didn't seem convinced. "Are you sure?"

"Look, Wade, I don't have much pride left. Let me retain what little dignity I can."

"I'm sorry. I didn't mean to make you uncomfortable."

His chagrin gave Leah the chance to find her humor again. "I admit, most women have a fantasy about falling down with January through June from the *Hunk-of-the-Month* calendar rushing to their aide. Unfortunately all my slips have been a little more ignoble."

Wade's humor returned, too. "So I don't qualify for hunk of the month? I'm crushed."

Leah felt her stomach clench. Hunk of the month? Hardly. Hunk of the year? Hands down. For the thousandth time, she told herself she wasn't supposed to be attracted to a client. Unfortunately her insides didn't seem to be receiving the signal from her brain.

She accepted Wade's hand to help her stand and tried to tell herself as he patted the dirt from her jeans that he'd do the same thing with Myra Jo. So, really, there was no need for her to go all foolish just because her thighs now felt as though they were on fire.

When he dusted her behind, she nearly fell again. She jumped far more than the touch deserved, even as his fingers moved to her shirt. She didn't dare let him near any cloth thinner than denim, for surely he'd feel the fever in her skin and the blood pounding in her chest.

"Uh...thank you, Wade. I'm fine now. Just fine."

She knew she sounded like the very idiot she'd prayed she wouldn't make of herself, but she couldn't help it. She made a show of shaking off the rest of the dust so she wouldn't have to look at him.

Myra Jo reacted first when they finally entered the house.

Running to her father, she hugged him and gave him a smacking kiss on the cheek. Leah received a less enthusiastic but decidedly warm hug, minus the kiss.

"Leah," Wade said, commanding her attention. "This is Jonathan, my baby brother."

She shook hands with the man who could have been formed from the same mold as Wade, just a bit stockier in the body, with hair that tended toward auburn instead of Wade's midnight black.

"Ma'am," Jonathan said, and all but tipped an imaginary hat.

What was it with these Mackey men? she wondered. Was there a cowboy chromosome on their DNA strand that she didn't know about? An X, Y and a horseshoe, maybe?

Jonathan's grin was warm and genuine, and there was more than mere polite interest in his deep blue eyes. She waited for her heart to quicken, something one might expect when a handsome man smiled with high-wattage power, and was amazed when her pulse remained unaffected.

"It's nice to meet you. Myra Jo said she had a—" Leah tapped her chin with a manicured nail "—let's see, how did she put it? Killer cute uncle, I believe she said."

Jonathan let out a deep laugh, delightful crinkles appearing at the corners of his eyes. "Why, thank you, ma'am. You'd best stop, though, or you'll put me to blushing."

A glance in Wade's direction caught her off guard, making her amusement fade. His expression was fierce, and she felt her face flush, as though she'd been caught with her hand in the cookie jar. She welcomed the return of irritation. Things had been getting a bit too intimate, anyway.

The odd moment dissipated when a woman Leah guessed to be about sixty-five came into the room. Common sense told her this was the Mackey matriarch. Time had taken its toll on the petite, gray-haired lady, but the warmth of her eyes and the spontaneity of her smile made up for any lack of classical beauty.

"Grams, this is Leah Houston," Myra Jo jumped in, taking Leah's hand and pulling her forward. "Leah, Grams."

"Please call me Joleen," the older woman insisted right off the bat.

"Only if you call me Leah."

"That'd be just fine. Now, sit down and tell me what I can get you to drink. Father will be down shortly."

Leah took one of the bar stools stationed around an oversize island in the middle of the kitchen. The room was a cook's dream. A stove was centered on one side of the island so Joleen could cook and talk to her family while they sat around the other three edges. Now Leah fully understood what Wade had meant when he'd said Joleen was in her glory when she was cooking.

A return look at Wade found him studying her. She shifted uncomfortably, as he seemed to be reading her thoughts. From Wade's good-ol'-boy demeanor and his warning about his father, she'd been expecting a version of the Clampetts, not an average Southern home. She hadn't meant to stereotype, but in this case, her imagination had been primed.

"Your kitchen is wonderful, Joleen."

"Lordy, yes, and I love it. Wade and Jonathan built this house for me and Father, and it means the world to me. We'll have to take you on a tour, but first I'm going to get busy with lunch. I put a ham in before we left for church, so give me a minute and we'll have us a bite to eat."

Leah took the stool Wade held out for her and chatted amiably with Joleen and Jonathan. When Mr. Mackey walked into the room a few moments later, it was all Leah could do to keep breathing as warning bells began ringing madly in her brain.

Wade and Jonathan must have taken after their mother's side of the family, she noted, because except for height, they bore little resemblance to the Scandinavian bear of a man who entered the room. His hair was light, almost white blond, and his eyes were the palest blue she'd ever seen. His very entrance denied his quiet step, for his presence was almost palpable.

So maybe Wade and his father weren't quite so different after all....

But what disconcerted Leah were the tears gathering behind her eyelids. Mr. Mackey looked so much like her grandfather that he could have been Grandaddy's brother. Except Grandaddy had been an only child, so no quirk of fate there.

Everything about Mr. Mackey made vivid, visceral images of her grandfather explode in her mind. He carried himself with the same pride, the same bearing, saying more clearly than words that he was a man who took guff from no one. Yet he somehow conveyed that life had taught him how to be gentle, too. A keen intelligence lurked in his ice blue eyes. Looking at Mr. Mackey made her heart wrench with longing for the grandfather who had died much too early. She missed him so badly, especially when she needed someone to talk to who understood her, accepted her and the decisions she'd made for her life and who'd always had the most sage advice to offer in his gruff but gentle voice.

Another similarity with Wade became apparent when she finally noticed Mr. Mackey's attire. His faded jeans weren't in the best repair, but they were clean, and the flannel shirt he had buttoned over a T-shirt had long ago faded from whatever shade of red the maker had given it. Still, it was tucked in neatly.

"Oh, great," Leah heard Myra Jo whisper. "First Daddy was a hard case, now Gramps."

Jonathan tried to console his niece. "Don't worry, sweetheart. Everything will be fine."

Leah managed to keep a polite mask while the introductions were made, but the warning meter in her head redlined.

The hand that shook hers gave no acknowledgment to two heart attacks and surgery. It was firm and warm and completely gentlemanly.

"Miss Leah," he said, tipping his head as Jonathan had done.

"Please, Mr. Mackey, I've gone through this with the whole family. Call me Leah."

"Well then, Miss Leah, are you a republican or a democrat?"

He had joined her at the island by now, taking the seat on the short end to her right. She took advantage of the time he took to settle himself to reclaim her equilibrium.

She decided the court should delete her prior statement from the transcript. Wade was exactly like his father.

"Um, I vote for the candidate, not the party."

"What's your favorite football team?"

She caught a twinkle in his eye that she was sure he hadn't planned for her to see, and her sense of humor returned.

"College or pro?" she rejoined with a raised eyebrow.

As he fought a smile, she realized that by the time this was over, negotiating the "Hatfields and McCoys" was going to seem like a walk in the park.

Four

Wade watched Leah field a barrage of personal questions from his family. If they became too personal, he would step in, but until then, he was letting her fight her own battles. After all, she had to learn what she was getting into.

He hated to admit it, but she was good at this. Maybe they did stand a snowball's chance in hell of getting through this wedding without fists flying. After all, if Leah could charm Earl Mackey, she could surely handle Bradford on his worst day.

He hid a smile as she caught him looking at her. He saw an odd mixture of amusement and weariness in her warm, melted-chocolate eyes. With the possible exception of himself, the Mackey clan was blessed with vibrant personalities and overdosed with curiosity, which was often overwhelming to the uninitiated.

The more he thought about it, the more he was sure a man could get lost in those dark brown eyes. They had captured him the moment he'd seen her all done up in one of her expensive suits he'd come to think of as her battle armor. She'd looked as though a steamroller couldn't bend her perfect posture. Yet while she'd handed out orders, she'd also handed out encouraging words to the nervous bride and groom, and even kept the bridesmaids and groomsmen in line. He'd been impressed.

He stopped his errant thoughts with a reminder that no matter how physically attractive, Leah was the last person he needed to get involved with. His relationship with Ysabel notwithstanding, he had learned the hard way about being involved with someone too different from him in ideals and ambitions.

He was an anachronism and he admitted it. He wanted an old-fashioned wife, one who wanted to be a part of his world, who enjoyed the country life. He had no desire for a wife who wanted a fast-track career or craved the glitzy social scene. And since he knew today's women would think him a caveman at best, he kept his opinions to himself.

Not that he was looking at Leah as wife material, of course. It was just easy to let his thoughts wander as he met her eyes across his parents' kitchen.

Was it so wrong for him to want a wife who would work with him to create a home, *their* home? A woman who wanted to be there when he came in after a long day's work, as anxious to see him as he was to see her? A woman who wanted the ranch to succeed because it was theirs, because they were partners, not because it was a ticket into the Texas social whirl?

"So how do you keep up with them all?"

He felt an odd disappointment when Leah wrenched her eyes away from his, and turned to Myra Jo.

"I'm sorry," she said, "what did you ask me?"

"All your brothers and sisters and nieces and nephews. I can't imagine trying to keep up with them all."

His daughter's question didn't surprise him. Being an only child, large families were something of an enigma to her.

Leah's laugh, a sort of husky chuckle, sang deliciously along his spine. "Well, after my father died, my job changed from merely being bossy to being a drill sergeant. My mother worked two jobs, and since I was the oldest, it was basically my responsibility to keep everyone and their schedules straight."

"Sounds like you had it rough, honey," Joleen said, sympathy turning her hazel eyes almost blue. His mother always had been a softie, even though she tried to act tough.

Leah's shrug looked a little forced. "Oh, sometimes, but it gave me great training for my career." She gave Myra Jo a playful punch on the arm. "I can keep a roomful of young women in line better than the toughest marine in the corps."

The answering chuckles were as much in response to Leah's attempt to lighten the mood as from Myra Jo's dramatic roll of her eyes. And if there was anything his daughter had mastered, it was the art of eye rolling.

Then Leah smiled, and her face turned from beautiful to breathtaking. With her hair pulled back in a long braid, she looked ten years younger than her business persona. Her smile lit her eyes, and her whole face glowed. She seemed as excited as a schoolgirl with a juicy secret to share when she turned back to Myra Jo.

"The shipment of gowns I was telling you about came in yesterday. I ordered three of them with you in mind, so you need to come in soon. You're running out of time, you know."

Myra Jo reached for his arm, and Wade was startled at how cold her hand was. "Can we go tomorrow, Daddy?"

"I'm sorry, baby, but I'm going down to Mexico to meet with another breeder. I won't be back until Friday morning."

"But, Daddy, you heard Leah. I'm almost out of time. I want the perfect dress, and if we have to order one, we've got to do it now. I'm not postponing the wedding again...for any reason."

He cast a quick glance across the island and felt Leah's anger before she quickly covered it with her professional mask. She probably thought the bull was just any one of a dozen dumb animals and could wait until after the wedding. She couldn't know this bull was part of his new plan to make his herd stronger. He had no intention of justifying his need to guarantee Myra Jo—and any grandchildren God might see fit to give him—would never face poverty. Oh, he didn't plan to give them the world on a silver platter, but he planned to make darn sure they had choices he hadn't had. This bull wasn't some petty hobby, but he'd be damned if he'd explain himself to anyone.

"I'm sorry, honey, I can't do it. I'll try to cut the trip short, and we can go on Thursday."

Myra Jo's chin took on a set, and she took her arm away from his.

"Don't bother. I'll pick out my gown myself if it's not important to you. Leah, would two o'clock Tuesday be okay?"

"Absolutely."

"Baby—"

Myra Jo stood and ignored him. "Thanks for lunch, Grams. It was wonderful. I'll see you later."

She left with a general goodbye to the room, and Wade made sure no hint of his feelings showed. Let them think he was a hard-hearted bastard. God knew he'd done enough to make Myra Jo angry with him, but he'd succeeded in delaying the wedding a full six months, hadn't he? Maybe he still had time to make Myra Jo see some sense. She'd forgive him in time. He hoped.

He suspected he was the only one who knew Leah wished she were just about anywhere else. Not surprisingly, his mother recovered her equilibrium and offered second helpings, adding a censuring frown when she handed him the potatoes.

Wade escorted Leah out a short time later, their exit having decidedly less drama than Myra Jo's. It was obvious his mother was thoroughly enchanted with the latest addition to the wedding frenzy, and his father had even given Leah a rare grin.

Maybe she knew it, maybe she didn't, but the smartest thing Leah had done all day was to not back down from his father.

When they reached the horses, she hesitated to step into his cupped hands to help her up. At his place she'd had a rock to use, but she couldn't mount here without assistance. His dad's grassy yard didn't provide any convenient boosters.

"Um, I appreciate the offer," she said, looking pointedly at his still-clasped hands, "but I can't—"

"Come on, Leah, it's only a short ride back. Thumper didn't treat you so rough, did she?"

"No, she didn't."

He straightened, and with the sun out of his eyes he could see she was blushing furiously. "I know you're a city girl, but are you that sore?"

Her blush intensified. Wade was so used to speaking his mind and hearing others on the ranch do the same, it never occurred to him a tender behind would traumatize her so badly.

"No, I—" She struggled to swallow and turned her back to him, patting Thumper's neck awkwardly and pushing Myra Jo's hat harder onto her head.

He waited. She was obviously fighting with herself, and he figured it'd be best if he stayed out of the way.

When she straightened her shoulders and turned around, the laughing Leah he'd watched a few moments before was gone, replaced by the Leah who was no-nonsense.

"It's nothing you've done, Wade. I'm simply too heavy for you to boost up. If you'll help me find a rock as I did at your place, I'll be fine."

No blush marred her cheeks. It was as if a shutter had come over her eyes, hiding any hint of embarrassment. She spoke as though her revelation was no big deal, but he hadn't been born yesterday. He'd heard the catch in her voice before she'd turned around, but God help him, he'd never thought she'd be upset. He'd helped people much bigger than she mount a horse and he hadn't thought twice about it.

"Leah, forgive me. I've helped so many folks onto horses, I never thought I'd embarrass you. As for you being too heavy, well, it's just plain stupid. Now come on, up you go."

Her cool persona stayed firmly in place as she reluctantly gave in and allowed him to assist her. It wasn't until they were almost at his house before she spoke again, and it was clear she was still in consultant mode.

"Wade, I understand you're a businessman, but your daughter is asking you to be with her to pick out her gown. Since her mother won't be there, I would think you'd be more sensitive."

He tried not to snap. "I said I'd go with her."

"But only on your terms. You've obviously forgotten, but I'll be here on Thursday, getting ready for the barbecue on Friday. Afterward, it's two short weeks to the rehearsal. There are a number of things hinging on you, you know."

As a matter of fact, he had forgotten about the damned barbecue. Most likely wishful thinking.

"I wasn't aware your bill included psychotherapy."

"Sometimes it's part and parcel of the job."

"Give me a discount then, because I don't need it—from you, or Myra Jo. If Myra Jo chooses not to wait until Thursday, then there's nothing I can do about it."

He noted she waited for him to help her dismount this time, undoubtedly willing to stand his touch rather than end up on her backside. Not that she hadn't looked incredibly appealing all sprawled out at his feet, but he doubted she'd see it that way.

Even though he could feel her frustration with him radiating from her, he had the strongest urge to pull her into his arms and kiss her until she was as confused and off balance as he was. Damn it, he didn't want to be affected by this woman. He didn't need the hassle, and he didn't have the time. She was here to coordinate a wedding, not field his advances.

He nearly laughed out loud at his foolishness. It was all well and good to give himself these little speeches, but every time he caught the sun glinting off the warm brown silk of her hair, striking red highlights in the pieces daring enough to escape from her braid, his fingers itched to free it all and fan the beautiful mass over her shoulders. Then his gaze would slip to her full lips, and his mouth would water at the thought of seeing if her lip gloss tasted as good as his imagination said it would.

When she cleared her throat, he realized he'd been staring.

"I'll see you on Friday, when you get back," she said in the most businesslike tone he'd heard from her yet. She handed him Myra Jo's hat.

"I reckon so."

He turned toward the corral with the horses in tow as she walked to her car.

He stopped and called out across the yard. "Take care of my baby, okay?"

Even with the distance between them, he saw her eyes soften.

"I will."

Leah could see Wade unsaddling the horses as she got into her car and started the engine, blessing the cool air soon blasting out of the vents.

Stubborn fool, she thought with mixed emotions as she watched his body move with a lithe, masculine grace. She wished he was the kind of guy who liked to work without a shirt, because she wouldn't have minded a glimpse of the muscled chest and taut stomach she'd gotten an all-too-brief view of the morning of the luncheon. He obviously went shirtless occasionally, since his skin was tanned a mouth-watering golden color, but he didn't seem obliged to give her another peek today.

She lost sight of him when he took a saddle into the barn. Her lustful thoughts faded into irritation toward him for not putting this wedding ahead of a stupid bull. Yet, from the hurt he'd quickly hidden at Myra Jo's cold exit, she guessed there was something important about this trip or he would have canceled it with no qualms.

Well, she was never going to figure it out in the blistering sunshine. Slipping her sunglasses on, she put the car in gear and headed back to Austin.

Tuesday arrived before Leah was ready. She had the bridal gowns steamed and ready for Myra Jo's arrival, but the mountain of work on her desk mocked her futile attempts to get the day's tasks accomplished.

The store—both stores in fact—had been insane. June not only seemed to be the favorite month for brides, but there must have been some unseasonable weather keeping folks inside last September if the number of little ones next door getting decked out for summer was any indication. Although most of the brides were picking up their orders, not trying gowns on, it didn't lessen the workload. Between the brides who had starved themselves a size smaller and the ones who had chocolate-caked themselves a size larger, the last-minute alterations were often as nerve-racking as selecting the gown in the first place.

Not for the first time today, she wondered why she stayed in this business.

A knock at her door startled her out of her negative mood. Seeing Myra Jo's beautiful face, so hopeful and yet so wary, made Leah determined to be charming and make the afternoon as special for Wade's daughter as she could.

Myra Jo preceded her beau into the office, and Leah rose to shake Pennington's hand.

"I'm delighted we've finally been introduced. Congratulations."

"Thank you, ma'am. I'm sorry I wasn't able to meet you sooner."

Myra Jo's laughter contained a good bit of irony as she cut a glance up at Penn. "I don't think most people wait this long to plan a wedding this big. I'm just glad Leah was willing to come to our rescue."

"Me, too."

Pennington turned the full effect of his smile on Leah— just like the one that had won his father several reelections. Except, in the son's case, there seemed no calculation behind the effortless charm.

"So...do you think I could stay and watch?"

Myra Jo's blush was delightful. "You just hush and come back around four o'clock."

"Yes, ma'am," he teased her, making her blush deepen.

Leah was charmed. No matter what anyone said, there was no doubting the love radiating from the tall, fair-haired man down to his tiny, bride-to-be. With Penn in a classic

black Pierre Cardin tuxedo, and Myra Jo in the dress Leah
was sure she'd pick, they were going to make an enchanting
couple.

After chatting for a moment or two, Leah shooed the
reluctant man out of the boutique and led Myra Jo down
the hall to the viewing room.

"Did...um...my dad call?"

Leah forced a smile. "No, honey, I'm sorry. He didn't."

Myra Jo nodded, managing to keep a pleasant expression
in spite of the obvious disappointment in her eyes. Leah
was beginning to worry about the petite young woman. She
was a tad too pale for Leah's comfort, but Myra Jo didn't
give her a chance to voice her concern.

"I brought my heels," Myra Jo said, lifting the evidence
for Leah to see. "Let's start playing dress up."

Myra Jo gasped when she entered the bridal room, her
expression awed as she walked toward the five dresses
waiting on mannequins. Leah loved clients like Myra Jo—
no pretend boredom, no implication it was Leah's job to
satisfy them, rather than give them the opportunity to make
themselves happy.

"If you want to see any of these on a real body before
you get started, one of my staff over in the Babies department is about your size."

"No," Myra Jo said a little distractedly as she fingered
the hand-tatted lace on Leah's favorite of the collection. "I
love this one, and the second from the right caught my eye,
as well. Number four has possibilities, but I think I'd rather
just try them on."

Leah was thrilled to see a renewed sparkle in Myra Jo's
eyes and agreed when she decided to save the best dress
for last. Leah helped Myra Jo into a body slip to make sure
no fabric snagged against her skin when she tried on number four.

The heels were actually low satin pumps, which Leah

applauded. The minimal advantage a high heel would give the diminutive young woman would not be worth the discomfort, and would do little to lessen the dramatic difference between Penn's height and her own.

When they had smoothed the formfitting dress around Myra Jo's hips, there was no question the classic A-line, with minimal augmentation, was a beautiful creation. The high, pearl-trimmed collar graced her slender throat, but after a quick turn in front of the mirror, Myra Jo didn't even ask for the veil.

Leah chuckled as she undid the hidden zipper, providing Myra Jo just enough room to wriggle out. "I didn't really think you'd pick this one, but every bride wants a range to choose from."

"Oh, it's lovely. And if I were six feet tall, it would look great. But since I'll never see the shy side of five-two, much less five-eleven, I think I have to pass on this one."

Leah slipped the dress back onto the mannequin while Myra Jo brushed a few loose hairs away from her face.

Dress number two merited more than a casual consideration, but they both knew the antebellum hoop just wasn't right.

The two women shared a giggle as Myra Jo bounded over to her first choice. The moment softened as she stroked the exquisite lace, and her eyes turned dreamy. Leah watched the changing expression and felt something she'd never felt before.

Envy.

Of all the ladies, young and not so young, she'd helped over the years, Leah had never felt anything out of the ordinary as she'd watched the process. But looking at Myra Jo, Leah was struck with the knowledge of never having had a similar expression on her own face when thinking about a lover. She didn't want to face the thought that she'd consistently picked men who wouldn't ask her to sacrifice much of herself. In her dreams, she pictured a strong man who wanted more than little pieces of her time, but in the cold light of day, she'd avoided men like...like Wade...who would demand more than just time with her body. He would claim a piece of her heart, body and soul.

Looking at this young lady, on the verge of a whole new phase of her life—standing there with such hope, such assurance that her future would be wonderful—was eye-opening to Leah. She felt hot tears building before she could stop them. She didn't usually indulge in self-pity. It was a foolish waste of time. And to envy this young girl for her good fortune was positively awful.

Her lack of a husband was inconsequential, Leah reminded herself. She wasn't exactly a femme fatale, but neither was she a celibate, although a glance at the calendar would reveal she was getting awfully close to qualifying for the latter. She couldn't remember the last date she'd had with Brandt. Their schedules just hadn't meshed lately. And she refused to consider that she was more relieved than upset.

I don't need a man cluttering up my life, she assured herself, ignoring the rather defensive tone of voice in her head.

Myra Jo returned from exchanging the hoop for a more sedate petticoat to gently flare the yards of ivory satin around her slender hips. When the dress was in place, Leah hushed her mind as she slipped the loops over the satin-covered buttons on the sleeves and down the back. She led Myra Jo to a cushioned stool where she could perch without crushing her dress, and began brushing Myra Jo's hair back smoothly. She gave it a simple twist before pinning the coil up and placing the veil frame over Myra Jo's forehead. A teardrop pearl on the inverted point gave the veil an exotic touch, and Leah was sure she had never seen a more beautiful bride.

She met Myra Jo's eyes in the mirror, and for a moment Leah couldn't breathe. All she could do was look at Myra Jo's lovely face and feel an ache reminding her she would never do this with her own child. She'd had the intellectual realization for years, but never felt this heart-clenching knowledge that the choice she'd made to favor a career over a family kept this opportunity out of reach. Leah didn't regret her path—it was one she'd walked willingly. But in this instant she felt a sense of loss such as she'd never known.

The distant sound of the bell ringing over the front door interrupted their stare. Leah regained her composure by arranging the veil's tulle bow, unable to express how grateful she was for this chance to be more than just a consultant to Myra Jo. Myra Jo was a bride without a mother, and Leah was a pseudo mother of the bride without a child.

"Ready?" Leah asked, smiling with anticipation. She could hardly wait to see Myra Jo's face when she finally saw the full effect.

Myra Jo nodded. She walked up the steps to the mirrors and fiddled with the lay of the skirt as if she were anticipating the moment as much as Leah, and hesitating on purpose.

Just as she raised her eyes to the mirror, the door to the room opened and she saw her father in the reflection. Leah watched the unspoken messages pass across the room, and tears again filled her eyes as Myra Jo tugged up the skirt to run into her father's arms.

"I'm sorry I'm late, baby."

"It's okay. We've just been playing up to now. Oh, Daddy, thank you for coming back."

A red smudge colored both cheeks as Wade walked with his daughter back to the platform. The picture they created was amusing, with Myra Jo in her finery and Wade dressed in clean but well-worn jeans, a white shirt, a straw cowboy hat and boots that hadn't seen a polishing cloth in years.

Leah motioned him to take a seat and joined him on the comfortable couch placed for the viewers.

"Oh, Leah, this is wonderful," Myra Jo breathed as she turned so she could see the dress from all sides. The Queen Anne neck was the perfect cut, and the leg-of-mutton sleeves were just the right touch. A little tuck in the waist and of course adjusting the length were the only alterations required.

"What do you think, Daddy?" she asked, twirling around gracefully.

"Baby, you look…I think…I mean…oh, damn, honey, you're the prettiest thing I've ever seen."

The joy on the daughter's face and the wonder in the father's answered Leah's earlier question to herself. This was why she stayed in the business. These rare moments when her clients were there for more than a show, when they truly wanted to make a dream come true, made her job pure joy.

Leah called in her seamstress and took advantage of the distraction to talk to Wade.

"I'm so glad you came. Myra Jo is so excited," she said softly, still looking at the stage. When he didn't respond, she moved her gaze to his and found his expression intent.

It disconcerted her. For once she couldn't tell what a customer was thinking. Of course, Wade wasn't a customer, per se, but at this stage of the game she usually could tell what the parents were thinking, as well as the bride.

Wade, on the other hand, was once again defying her experience. She knew he thought his daughter was beautiful; that had been obvious. But there had been a subtle underplay of emotions chasing themselves like shadows across his features. His tense posture told her he was battling himself, and she assumed it was because he was truly caught between his principles and his love for his daughter. He wanted to give her the moon, but she was still asking for something much more valuable.

At least Leah assumed he was thinking something of the sort. For all she knew he could be planning his herd rotation.

"Thank you for doing this for Myra Jo."

"You're welcome, although it wasn't as special until you came in."

"Oh, I don't know about that. This is one of those women's moments, I think, and she needed a woman's hand."

Leah impulsively put her hand on his forearm. "I'm glad I could be here for her. She's become very special to me."

When he covered her fingers with his own, the warmth of his touch sent shivers shooting up her arm.

How did this man manage to make her react so strongly to his merest look? She didn't like feeling discombobulated, and Wade seemed to have a particular knack for it. She sometimes enjoyed the stomach-clenching excitement of a tough negotiation, but she was feeling baffled, which was not the same at all.

It struck her that for the first time she was feeling a true sense of grief for her choices. Wade was the first man who had ever made her think about marriage and babies and white picket fences. She wanted to resent him for affecting her so, but the tender ache in her heart didn't leave room for anger.

"So, Daddy, how'd the trip go?"

Leah sent Myra Jo a silent thank-you for saving her from her troubled thoughts.

"Fine."

Myra Jo sighed, and Leah contained a smile as their eyes met. They both were thinking the same thing: men!

"Did you get the bull you wanted?"

"Nope."

"Daddy..." Myra Jo said in a tone she could only have learned from her father.

Wade had the grace to look sheepish. "We couldn't agree on the terms, so I said I'd get back with him after the wedding."

Myra Jo went still and stared at her father. "You cut short a negotiation to come back? For me?"

Wade fidgeted with his hat. "Of course I did, honey. Actually," he cleared his throat and turned the hat once more, "I was kinda wishing I hadn't gone in the first place."

Leah looked at him in astonishment. She had been sure the last thing Myra Jo would ever get was an apology, even a quasi one. The man never ceased to amaze her.

When the seamstress finished, there was nothing left to do but shoo Wade out of the room and help Myra Jo back into her street clothes. In minutes they joined Wade in the foyer and hardly had time to reestablish a conversation before the door opened and Penn came in.

Leah watched the dynamics of the room shift, and she wanted to strangle Wade. The afternoon had been wonderful, and now the strained look was back on Myra Jo's face. Wade was certainly polite to Penn, but the temperature seemed to have dropped several degrees.

She decided to step in.

"Hello again, Penn. I want you to know your bride picked an incredible dress."

Penn looked down at Myra Jo, who stood beside him with her arms almost protectively wrapped around him. "I knew she would. But then, she'd look beautiful in a burlap sack."

"Yeah, but burlap itches," Myra Jo said, trying for a lighter note.

"Is everybody ready for the barbecue Friday?" Leah asked, hoping her voice wasn't too bright.

"Yes, ma'am," Penn said, either missing or ignoring the straightening of his future father-in-law's shoulders. "We're looking forward to it."

Wade cleared his throat. "Thank you for your time today, Leah, but I've got to get back out to the ranch." He turned to Myra Jo. "Will I see you later?"

"I'm having dinner with Penn and his parents, so if it gets too late, I'll just stay at Penn's."

Leah could almost hear Wade's muscles freezing solid. She was proud, though, when he merely nodded one sharp bob of his head and walked out.

"Myra Jo," Penn admonished gently, "you know your dad doesn't like to know when you stay at my place. You should have told him you were staying with a girlfriend."

"I'm not going to lie, Penn. I love Daddy, but I love you, too, and I'm not ashamed of my behavior."

"Hey, you two lovebirds," Leah interrupted, as they had obviously forgotten her presence, "you'd better get along. I'm sure you have a hundred errands to run."

Penn and Myra Jo jumped, and looked sweetly embarrassed.

"Thanks for everything," Myra Jo said, moving to give Leah a hug. "I'm going to bring Grams in tomorrow to pick out a new dress. Is that okay?"

"Of course it is. I'll be sure to be here."

"That'd be terrific. Grams really likes you."

"I like her, too. But you quit worrying so much. Just relax and enjoy yourself, okay?"

Penn forwent a hug to shake her hand. "I'll make her rest, don't worry. And thanks for taking care of my girl."

As she watched them walk down the sidewalk, Leah couldn't help but note that Wade had said much the same thing. Funny, everyone wanted Myra Jo taken care of, but no one seemed to be asking Myra Jo what she wanted.

Unable to face the mound of work on her desk after such

a touching afternoon, Leah decided to walk over to the Babies side and see how things were going.

As she'd expected, the charming showroom was bustling with people. She spotted Rhonda helping a young woman holding a newborn and headed in their direction.

"Leah, come here. I want you to meet someone."

She looked up from her inspection of a christening gown made of the finest lawn. The lace was delicate and soft, and Leah was proud her shop carried such exquisite work.

She smiled at the young mother when she reached Rhonda's side.

"Hello, I'm Leah Houston."

Rhonda put her hand on the mother's arm. "This is my friend, Maggie, and her new son, Jordan."

"Congratulations," Leah said, reaching out to touch his tiny, perfect ear. "It's nice to meet you."

"And you." Maggie shifted her sleeping son. "Would you like to hold him?"

Leah was delighted to take the tiny bundle into her arms. This was her favorite part of visiting the Babies side. She could get a "kid fix" and then go back to her office.

She looked down at Jordan's precious face and smiled tenderly. What was it about a baby that could turn a stubborn, dedicated working woman into mush? She knew if Jordan was awake, she would be cooing in baby talk and making a fool out of herself. Except this was the one place she could do it and get away with it, which was why she indulged the urge on a regular basis.

The only problem was, it fueled Rhonda's certainty that someday she was going to meet the right man and want a baby. Leah had stopped trying to explain her lack of desire for a child of her own. Rhonda just could not understand that she'd felt trapped when she was a teenager. Trapped by her brothers and sisters, trapped by a responsibility that was awfully heavy for a young girl's shoulders. She'd

vowed she would never be tied down like that again. For
Rhonda, having children was her heart's desire, but Leah
was fully content showering affection on her nieces and
nephews. She was even sure she'd be a terrific grandparent,
but dreams of Wade notwithstanding, she'd never figured
out how to skip the part about getting married and having
a child first.

The bell chimed when the door opened, and Leah looked
toward the door. She smiled when she saw Tammy Griffen
walk in.

Leah chatted with Rhonda and Maggie, finally relinquishing the beautiful boy to his mother. She excused herself and went looking for Tammy, finding her in the newborn section.

"Tammy, what are you doing here?"

The younger woman whirled, her face flushing. "Ohmy-
gosh, Leah. You nearly scared me to death."

"I'm sorry. I didn't mean to. Who's having a baby
shower this week?"

"I'm not going to a shower, Leah. I'm pregnant."

"Congratulations! That's wonderful."

"Yeah, I'm really excited. But I'm not here to shop for
the baby. Yet. I tried to find you next door and they said
you were over here."

"Well, you found me. What can I do for you?"

"I wanted to try on my bridesmaid dress. My waist is
already thickening, and I haven't tried it on in weeks."

Leah smiled sympathetically. "No problem at all,
Tammy. The A-line of the dress will make a bit of tummy
easy to hide, not that you shouldn't be proud of your changing figure, though."

"Oh, I'm not asking because of vanity. I don't want
Myra Jo to know until she gets back from her honeymoon.
She's so stressed out, she would decide—here at the last
minute—that I couldn't be an attendant because I might

faint or something. I don't want to add any more pressure on her."

Leah hooked her arm around Tammy's shoulders and led her through the connecting hallway to the Brides side.

"You are such a sweet friend. I know Myra Jo will be so excited for you, but I think you're right. Let's wait until after the wedding is over."

Leah helped Tammy with her gown and tried to quiet the obnoxious voice inside her head that pointed out her double standard. She had been berating everyone else for protecting Myra Jo without consulting her, and now she was doing the same thing.

She wanted to believe her motives were entirely altruistic, but the little nagging voice didn't believe her.

Five

At the sound of Spoiled Rotten's bark, Wade turned from his work in the barn and glanced outside to see Leah's sporty red car coming down the long driveway. Her big company van was close behind. He hushed Rotten and started putting his tools away.

Part of him wanted to see her, part of him didn't, although he didn't care to define which parts were which. It was bad enough the woman had thrown him into a tailspin from the moment he'd met her. Now he couldn't forget the look on her face as she'd watched Myra Jo at the salon. He doubted Leah even knew her face had been glowing, filled with pride.

He still wasn't sure what he felt. His emotions were all tangled up—partly anger at Julie for being so coldhearted; partly joy at seeing Myra Jo radiant in her finery. And partly gratitude to Leah for her attention to his daughter, mixed with an inexplicable guilt for wishing she were Myra

Jo's mother. Mostly, though, he was baffled by the strength of his attraction to Leah, an attraction he had never felt—not for Julie, not for Ysabel, not for any woman he'd ever known.

More than that, he didn't want to analyze.

All he knew was his gut had clenched, and it had been all he could do to keep from yanking her into his arms and kissing her—right in front of his daughter—until Leah saw stars.

Now she sat in his driveway, and he had wasted his time lost in thought instead of heading for the house and a shower. At the moment, he looked like the redneck she probably thought him to be.

He had no need to impress Leah or anyone else, he assured himself defensively; it just wasn't proper for a man to welcome a lady dressed as he was.

Hurrying across the back lawn, he kicked off his boots and slipped into the house. He could hear Jonathan's laughter coming from the kitchen, so he knew his brother would take care of things until a shower turned him more presentable.

Leah turned off her engine after she pulled to a stop in Wade's driveway, something she felt she'd done a hundred times already. It was foolish to feel as though she'd come home every time she drove onto the Mackey ranch, and she scolded herself for the absurd thought.

Worse than absurd. The thought made her distinctly uncomfortable.

She did wonder, though, what had happened to time since she'd met Wade Mackey. It was already Thursday, and the Mackey barbecue was barely a day away. She'd always kept a hectic schedule, but it seemed time now flew by at hurricane speed. She could hardly catch a deep breath. Or maybe the phenomenon had started when Wade kissed her. The memory of his mouth on hers had not lessened one tiny bit.

She caught herself licking the fullness of her bottom lip where he'd nipped it so gently, yet so arousingly, and pulled herself up short. She was not going to behave this way.

She was proud she managed not to think about Wade every second. Every other minute, perhaps, but all in all she was getting better. *This is just a business deal* had become her mantra. She had everything but her silly heart convinced the kiss by Town Lake had been a fluke. She kept reminding her heart it was an organ, incapable of sending her disconcerting thoughts such as how incredibly sexy Wade was, or what a great kisser, or how much she'd like to be kissed by him once more.

As she glanced toward the barn, she wished for the first time in her career she could have canceled or rescheduled the wedding that Rhonda was coordinating tomorrow. If they hadn't been double-booked, she would have postponed facing Wade until the wedding itself—because she most certainly would have chickened out and sent Rhonda to do the barbecue. She might have felt like a heel, but she still would have done it. Her control of her mental functions when she was within ten feet of Wade Mackey was tenuous at best.

Leah reset her grip on her steering wheel and gave herself a stern warning to get herself together. She needed to get her mind off Wade's tight, sexy behind and onto her strategy for the party tomorrow. She had no control over how the guests mixed and mingled, but her deliberate plans for outdoor and indoor seating would keep the Mackeys and the Bradfords relatively segregated and minimize the chances for the exchange of angry words.

Texas chic would be the dress of choice, so Leah didn't have to worry about tuxedos—yet. She was still stymied as to how she was going to get Wade in a tux. The man was nothing short of mule-stubborn, but she could put the dilemma aside for the weekend. She knew Wade could handle dressing country...an understatement if she'd ever thought one.

Jonathan greeted her at the back door as though she were a long-lost friend. She was so amused she forgot to be offended when he pulled her into a spontaneous bear hug. When he released her and stepped back, she wondered—not for the first time—why Rhonda twitched every time she mentioned Wade's brother. As far as she could tell, both men were cut from the same charming, Southern-mannered cloth, although Jonathan was certainly the more extroverted of the two. She made a mental note to grill Rhonda when a spare moment presented itself.

"So, have you been behaving yourself since Sunday?" she asked, allowing Jonathan to put his arm around her waist as he escorted her to the huge den she would soon transform to seat twenty or thirty people.

"Aw, that wouldn't be any fun, now would it?" he countered, stepping back to let Leah's two helpers through to place folded tables against the wall.

"Myra Jo has gone shopping," Jonathan said after insisting on lending a hand. "She'll be back later this evening."

Since she didn't need Myra Jo at this stage, Leah hoped the young woman would enjoy herself and maybe relax a little. She was soon too busy helping move furniture and hauling in the rest of the tables and chairs to worry about much else. The caterer would provide everything having to do with the food, so all she had to finish was the decorating. She started arranging tables and chairs while the men went for her supply crates.

She had been digging through her portfolio for a pen to begin her checklist when she felt a warmth on her neck.

She didn't have to look up to know who had just entered the room. She'd felt him on every nerve ending she possessed.

"Good evening," he said as he closed the distance between them.

She nodded, unable to push any words through her throat, struck dumb by the sight of him obviously fresh from the shower. And a shave, she noted from the still-red smoothness of his cheeks and a giveaway nick on his jaw. She had to clench her hands into fists to keep from brushing off the faint trace of shaving cream resting just behind his earlobe.

He smelled like shampoo and a light, citrusy cologne. His hair was damp, combed in his usual brushed-back style, but with a delightfully stubborn lock falling over his forehead.

Leah reclaimed her voice with an effort. "Jonathan and my guys should be back any second now."

An inordinate amount of time seemed to pass as they looked at each other, unable to move.

"I'll go help them then," Wade finally said, his voice low and carrying a reluctant quality which made her lightheaded.

"No need, Brother." Jonathan entered, carrying two huge crates. "We've got it all."

Leah took a breath of the air Jonathan seemed to have returned to the room, listening as he introduced her helpers, Andrew and Matthew, to Wade.

Just when Leah thought she was safe with the addition of three chaperons, Jonathan piped up.

"We're going to take a break," he said in her direction, only to turn to Wade and ask, "Did you know this woman's a slave driver? We're going to escape while we've got a chance."

Alone again with Wade, Leah was determined to ward

off the awkwardness she felt by opening the crates and sorting out the decorations. She was doing just fine until Wade moved beside her to start on the next box. The sleeveless shirt she'd chosen for freedom of movement suddenly felt inadequate, and the fine hairs on her arms tingled with an almost electric awareness.

She wished he wouldn't stand so close. It made her hands unsteady, and she seemed to drop everything onto the table instead of placing things.

Wade cleared his throat, startling Leah into looking up.

"Leah, you'll need to act as my hostess tomorrow night."

She was sure she hadn't heard him correctly. His voice was gruff, and his face held a frown—hardly the expression of someone asking a favor. But then, she reminded herself, he hadn't asked. He'd told her what he wanted her to do. Wade Mackey didn't ask for favors. He didn't ask anything of anybody.

"Hostess?"

"That's what I said. You and I both know it would be a disaster for me to greet everyone coming through the door, and I don't want Myra Jo doing anything more than she has to. She's looking awful peaked lately."

"I understand your dilemma, but I have to decline. It would be totally inappropriate for me to—"

"I wasn't asking. I'm making this part of your duties."

Now she was getting mad. She hadn't contracted for this and he wasn't God.

"And I said no. I'm not a member of the family or even a close friend. Your…request…is unacceptable."

"Who cares if you're a member of the family or not?"

"It is a common rule of etiquette. In fact, it's just common sense."

Wade snorted. "Then I think we have different definitions of common sense. And you know me well enough to know I don't give a horse's hind end about that kind of stuff. I've been honest from the beginning. I told you I needed someone who can handle the two-faced phonies of Bradford and his ilk.''

Leah was stunned at how much his implication hurt her. Did he mean he thought her two-faced because it was her job to smile in awkward situations and make even phonies feel comfortable?

"Don't worry, Wade. I do my best work with the pretentious.''

Wade looked irritated. "Leah, I didn't mean to insult you. I only meant you have experience in situations like this. Besides, I can tell you've grown attached to Myra Jo, and I was hoping you'd do it for her.''

"First you imply I'm a mere step above your average hypocrite, then you play on my sympathies for your daughter. What's next, a bribe? Or better yet, a threat?''

"If I have to.''

Gone was any hint of sympathy or understanding. Now her fingers trembled in fury. She pivoted on her heels and headed for the door, knowing if she said one more word she'd regret it. She hadn't made it past the couch before he caught her and swung her around to face him.

"Leah, I—''

Yanking her arm out of his grasp, she stood toe-to-toe with him and glared up into his eyes. "You can go to hell.''

This time he didn't try to stop her...until his voice reached her as she neared the door.

"Leah, please stop.''

She did, but kept her back to him. She tried to close her heart to the unmistakable sound of a man who knew he'd screwed up, who was just as angry as she was, but who also loved his daughter enough to risk his pride. Not an easy feat for a man like Wade. Well, she had her pride, too, and it had already taken a beating from her inability to control her response to him and being insulted to the core.

"Please stay."

His apologetic tone earned him a reluctant turn and a glacial glare.

Wade ran his fingers through his hair and rubbed the back of his neck before looking up and motioning to the couch with one hand.

"Leah, I apologize. Please sit down and let's talk."

She nodded and moved stiffly to the other end of the sofa. He waited until she sat down before doing the same, shifting sideways so he could see her better.

He clasped his hands together in his lap and studied his thumbnails. "I've accepted I can't stop this wedding. No matter how much I might want to."

"It seems you'd want the barbecue to be a fiasco then. It's your last big chance to put a monkey wrench in the works."

Her voice was as cold as his eyes when he wrenched his head around to look at her. "Do you really think I'm such a bastard?"

No, she didn't. No matter how mad she was, she would have been shocked if he'd announced such a plan. But if they were going to clear the air, then damn it, they were going to do it.

"Are you?"

His jaw clenched so hard she wondered if he was going to crack a tooth.

"No matter what kind of plowboy you think I am, I'm not an imbecile. I'm a father who wants to protect his child. But I know a scene tomorrow would only hurt Myra Jo, not persuade her to cancel her plans. It would distance her from me, and possibly Penn from his parents. It's hard enough to start a marriage without being alienated from your in-laws.'' His fists tightened in his lap. "I should know."

She waited for him to stand and begin to pace. When he did, she found herself sadly amused to be right.

"Myra Jo's mother and I went to high school together. Her daddy was—is—the preacher at First Street Church. Julie was every bit the stereotyped PK. Being a preacher's kid is hard enough, but being an only child was even harder on her. I was seventeen and all hormones when Julie and I started dating."

He gave her a self-deprecating smile. "If you could call our usual evening together a date. Anyway, how we managed to last a whole year before Julie got pregnant is nothing short of a miracle. And just when I was about to go off to college, Julie broke the news—with her daddy right behind."

Wade moved to the chair across from Leah and sat, resting his elbows on his knees and dangling his hands between them.

"Julie's family seemed rather surprised that I didn't need a shotgun to make me do my duty."

He laughed dryly, and Leah could tell he still resented the implication, even after all these years.

"Besides," he continued, "my dad had a heart attack three months later, so I would have had to come home from college in any event. Julie was furious about the whole thing. She had never intended to tell me, or anyone else. She was planning on a trip to Dallas to visit a cousin and take care of the little nuisance, as she called it. Her father overheard her, ending her scheme, and we were married two weeks later. Myra Jo had barely started smiling before Julie was gone."

Wade met her eyes. "I'm all Myra Jo has ever had. I may be stubborn, and I may have tried to dissuade her from this marriage, but I will not embarrass her or hurt her."

Leah felt the last of her fury slipping away. She was hardly feeling warm and fuzzy, but at least she no longer wanted to slug him.

She assimilated what he'd told her. "So, with this miraculous change of heart, you're ready to do whatever it takes to make Myra Jo happy?"

"Within reason," he agreed slowly, eyeing her carefully. "And I didn't mean to insult you earlier. I'm not very practiced at this sort of thing."

She understood and actually gave him more credit than he knew. A man who loved his child as much as he did deserved lots of points. Even if he was stubborn and bullheaded and...

"I accept your apology. And you were correct—I have a lot of experience handling those stuffy types. It's the only part of my job I don't like."

"I can understand, but I'm still going to ask you to be my hostess tomorrow. If not for my sake, then Myra Jo's."

She gave him a warning look. "So now you're asking?" She held up a hand to cancel her jab. "You don't have to pull my emotional strings, Wade. I'll do it for you, and for Myra Jo."

Then she smiled. "Because you're right, I do have a fondness for your child. She seems to have reached in and grabbed my heart when I wasn't looking."

He smiled back, tension easing out of his body as his shoulders relaxed. "She has a way of doing that to folks."

"It's still going to be awkward," she warned. "You're going to get some very pointed questions thrown your way."

"I'm pretty good with ignoring unwanted questions—"

"I've noticed."

"—and besides, we can solve the etiquette problem right now."

He stood and was beside her, pulling her to her feet

before she figured out what he was doing. He kept her hands in his and placed a warm kiss on her cheek.

"There, problem solved. You are now an official friend of the Mackey family."

"Hey, you two," Jonathan boomed, coming into the room. "Cut that out."

Leah jumped back as though stung, avoiding the openly curious looks she received from Andrew and Matthew.

"We're finished outside," Jonathan offered. "All the tables and chairs are set, the Japanese lanterns are up, the stereo is wired. One tent is over the driveway, and the other is on the lawn. Oh, and the potted plants are artfully arranged."

She cast a look at her men, but they just shrugged and grinned. They weren't stupid. If a guy as strong as Jonathan wanted to help them, who were they to argue?

"Great, I guess you're done then."

Needing no further urging, Andrew and Matthew were out the door with a smile and a "See you later, boss."

When they heard the back door slam, Jonathan's grin took on a wicked air. "So, just what were you two up to?"

"Not a thing," Leah answered breezily, returning to the decorations table.

"I was just making Leah an official friend of the family so she can play hostess tomorrow."

"Friend of the family, hmm?" Jonathan asked, raising one eyebrow.

Sauntering her way, he cast a mischievous grin at his brother. From beneath her lashes, Leah noted both his movement and a thunderous look from Wade, so she was ready to offer her cheek when he reached her side. She gasped instead when he took her shoulders and whirled her to face him.

"Then I claim a family welcome as well."

Only Jonathan didn't buss her cheek. He planted his

closed lips against hers in a brief, hard kiss. It only lasted a second, and although she knew she should be put out, all Leah could do was try not to laugh. Oh, she would bet Jonathan was a good kisser, but besides being pleasant, his embrace had none of the punch his older brother's had. Before she could put on a token protest, though, Wade pulled his brother away, and Leah was sure that cannibal chiefs would back down from his expression.

"Very funny, Jonathan."

Jonathan winked at her and faced his brother squarely. "Who was being funny? I walk into the room to see you kissing a gorgeous woman. You tell me she's an official friend of the family, so I figure, hey, I might as well make it official, too."

He held out his hand to Leah. "Welcome to the family," he said, raising both eyebrows and giving the slightest jerk of his head toward Wade as if to say, "What's with him?"

Leah burst out laughing, despite her efforts not to, and took the offered hand. "Thank you, Jonathan. You and Wade have now made me feel quite…welcome."

They exchanged conspiratorial grins and Jonathan backed away on light feet. "Well, I promised the munchkin I'd fix the cinch on her saddle, so I'll be in the barn. You two go on with what you were doing. I won't…um… interrupt again."

A low growl came from Wade's throat, but before any words followed, Jonathan was gone.

"That pup! I'll—"

"Oh, Wade, let it go. He was just having fun, and I took no offense." Deciding a change of topic was wise, she returned to her sorting and said, "Wade, thank you for sharing so much with me. Myra Jo is going to be thrilled you're giving up the fight."

His attention turned to his daughter, Wade promptly forgot about Jonathan. For now. Leah was sure Jonathan would be hearing more later.

"I hope so. I'm worried about her."

"I know, but it's just prewedding nerves. She's had a lot to do with graduating, preparing for a wedding and battling tooth and nail with her favorite daddy."

He winced. "Yeah, I guess I ladled a bit more on her plate than she needed."

"Don't berate yourself. Just let me take advantage of this momentary softening, and while I've got you in the compromising mood, let's talk about tuxes."

"Let's not."

"Wade," she said warningly when he moved toward the unopened crates. "Let's."

He started unpacking as though he hadn't heard her.

"I'm not going to let you ignore me."

Wade sighed and glanced heavenward. "Women," he muttered.

She folded her arms across her chest and tapped her nails on her elbow.

His face took on the mulish expression she was beginning to expect. "I've already said I'm not going to argue this anymore. That's about all the compromising a man can do in one day."

"But in light of all you've done, surely wearing a tuxedo seems like a minor inconvenience."

Wade put his hands on the table and leaned his weight on his arms. "No, Leah, it's not. I know this seems silly to you, but I won't get in a monkey suit for anyone, not even Myra Jo. I've worn one once, and I'll never do it again."

"I read the article, Wade. And I imagine what you're really mad about is the jab the reporter took at Myra Jo, right?"

He looked at her before nodding shortly.

"Then you need to ask yourself if you're more worried about your thick pride or about the reviews of your daughter's wedding. Because this wedding is going to make the society page, Wade. It's inevitable. And I don't think you want any comparisons to the previous incident."

His look was implacable. Knowing when to back off and change strategies, Leah tried for second best. "Okay, we'll drop the tuxedo issue for now. But may I see what you're going to wear tomorrow? Just for grins?"

He gave her a look telling her he was aware of her tactics. "I promise to leave my chewin' tobacky upstairs."

"Wade—"

He lifted his hand. "I know my daughter loves me, Leah. But I also know she wants me to be something I'm not. I'll never be a dandified city boy, but I'll show you my duds, if it'll make you happy. Just don't push me too far."

She took him at his word and followed him to his room without another word. The heady scent that was uniquely his hit her as he opened the door and turned on the light. The room was tidy, but somehow the neatly made bed didn't lessen the impact on her senses. She still felt the intimacy of the room, saw his stamp on everything from the pair of jeans with a belt still in them draped over the back of a chair, to the bookshelf that carried titles from *Horse Breeding for the Nineties* to the latest legal thriller. A leather-strapped watch lay on his dresser, one band lying flat, the other arching up to form an upside-down *U*. Several coins surrounded a walnut change bowl stamped with his initials. No doubt a present from Myra Jo, since Wade hardly seemed like the change bowl type.

Nothing particularly unusual, just a room with an essence singing to her like a siren's call.

Her perusal had only taken a few seconds. Thankfully, Wade had been rummaging in his closet and hadn't noticed her appraisal. By the time he turned around, she had re-gained her composure.

Laying dark, newly creased jeans on the bed, he added a starched white dress shirt, a tan belt and his dress boots from the closet. Like every other pair of boots he owned, they spoke of comfort and were well broken in, but these carried a high gloss from a recent shining.

Leah struggled with what to say. He was waiting for her approval, and she had to think fast. "What's Myra Jo wearing?"

"Myra Jo?" he parroted, obviously caught off guard.

"Petite, long, dark hair, lives here?"

"Very funny. I don't know."

"She didn't show off a new outfit for the event?"

He concentrated. "Come to think of it, she did. She got this skirt with three layers, and it looks like it's been stuffed in a drawer for a year, you know?"

"It's called broomstick pleating, and yes, I know. What color is it?"

He frowned again. "Mostly red with some blue and gold design on it."

"Okay, and her blouse?"

"It's a vest kind of thing. Like the one you've got on," he added. "But hers has a cutout that shows her throat. She's not tucking it in."

Leah contained a smile. "No, you don't tuck them in. What material is the shirt?"

"I don't know! But it's blue."

"Blue like navy or blue like blue jeans?"

"Like blue jeans."

"Okay then, here's the plan. I'll stop tomorrow and get you a new shirt and a belt. What's your waist size?"

"Thirty-four, but what do you mean get me a new shirt? What's wrong with this one?"

"Nothing. Do you have any ties?"

"Of course I have a tie, but I'm not wearing—"

"Can I see them—it?"

He opened the second closet door to reveal a rack mounted to the inside. He indeed owned one traditional tie—a horrible blue thing obviously purchased in the last decade. But as she suspected, she found several nice bolos. A silver faceted one on the end caught her eye and she pulled it out.

"This is beautiful. New?"

He nodded. "For Myra Jo's commencement."

"It suits you."

He blushed, something so rare she was fascinated.

"Well, Myra Jo picked it out."

"Then she has just as good taste in accessories as she does in fathers."

She moved back to the bed to keep him off guard. If he got his balance before she was ready, he might mess up her plan.

She laid the bolo on the white shirt and it was painfully obvious the outfit was a failure. Still, with the shirt she had in mind, and a braided black leather belt with a silver buckle, he'd look positively edible.

She felt herself flush. Wrong choice of words at this particular moment.

She cleared her throat. "This is great, Wade. Keep these boots and jeans, and I'll bring a shirt and belt—"

"Leah—"

She grabbed his wrist and gave him her most disarming smile. "Myra Jo is going to be so proud of you. You'll be the most handsome man here."

His smile started slowly and warmed her from her toes up. He moved his hand from beneath hers to capture her elbow in a gentle grip.

"So you think I'm handsome, huh?"

She hated the telling stain on her cheeks. "Well, I meant Myra Jo would...I mean..."

"Oh, I don't mind if you think it," he said, brushing the wisps of her bangs away from her face.

The room was suddenly suffocatingly small. She didn't know how they'd gone from a light, teasing moment to the desire she saw in his eyes, and her thoughts wouldn't stay coherent enough for her to form a hypothesis. The whys and wherefores suddenly didn't seem to matter. All she wanted was for him to kiss her.

His head began a slow descent to hers, his breath caressing her nose with the warm scent of peppermint.

"Wade—" she whispered.

"What?"

He didn't let her answer. Instead, he pulled her completely into the circle of his arms and claimed her lips possessively. It was a long, hot, drugging kiss, drawing at the very center of her. She knew she should protest and stop him before she lost herself completely, but there was no denying the headiness of his touch. He arched her further backward until her throat was exposed to the seeking nips of his teeth.

With his face buried in her neck, he breathed deeply.

"You smell so good," he said huskily, caressing the line of her jaw with the tip of his nose. "Like wildflowers after a spring shower, all warm and moist in the afternoon sun."

A rancher and a poet? She decided she should hardly be surprised. In fact, nothing about Wade should catch her off guard any more.

"Wade, we—"

"Shhh." He placed a fingertip on her lips before sliding the callused pad against the smoothness of her throat and down into the vee of her shirt. Her knees threatened to fail, and he obliged by pulling her with him onto the bed, unmindful of the clothes they'd just been examining.

The shock of landing fully on top of him, her breasts against his chest, her hips matched to his, took her breath away. But any awkward feelings vanished when he rolled her onto her back and took her mouth in a demanding mastery that left no doubt this was a man of passion, of deep masculine fires. And he wanted her with an undeniable fierceness.

He sent her senses reeling. She tossed her head from side to side as he devoured her with his kisses. His mouth was everywhere—on hers, on her throat, back to her mouth, her cheeks, her eyelids. She was lost in a maelstrom of sensations as he made quick work of the few buttons of her shirt. She felt the breeze from the ceiling fan on the heated flesh of her breasts straining against the confines of her bra, and nearly came out of her skin when his touch grazed one sensitive mound. She bucked against him when his thumb stroked over the heated lace.

"Whoa, there," he said with a thoroughly seductive, thoroughly male chuckle. Placing his hand on the fullness of her backside, he pulled her to him and arched her over his arm.

She wanted to tell him to stop, that this was wrong, but the only sounds coming from her throat as he unclasped the front hook of her bra were whimpers seeming to say, "Please. More."

He obliged, taking the weight of her breast into his free hand and teasing her taut nipple with the warm, wet tip of his tongue. Her mind completely left her then, abandoning her to only the sensation of fingers and teeth and tongue on her body. She dug her nails into his arms, holding on for dear life as he took her on a journey—

"Daddy?"

They both rose straight up out of the bed.

"Daddy?" Myra Jo repeated from down the hall.

Leah struggled with her clothes, mortified beyond words.

"Quick, the bathroom."

She raced for the door and shut it just as she heard Wade say, "Hi, honey. Home so soon?"

She hoped Myra Jo didn't notice the out-of-breath quality to Wade's voice, or anything else out of place. Or suspect why, if she did.

"Where's Leah? I saw her car outside."

Leah straightened her shirt and used Wade's brush to drag her disheveled hair away from her face. With speed born of desperation, she rebraided it and tied the end.

"She's in the bathroom. She'll be right out. We were…uh…she wanted to see what I'm wearing tomorrow."

Leah splashed cold water on her face and was dabbing it off with a towel as Myra Jo said, "Oh, good. Surely she's talked you out of that wrinkled shirt. The jeans are okay, though."

Leah opened the door and reentered the room. "Hi, Myra Jo. Did you find any bargains?"

"I found some great shoes and a new dress for the honeymoon. Want to see?"

"Sure, but why don't we go to your room?"

"I'll go get my packages and meet you there."

Wade and Leah looked at each other as Myra Jo disappeared, and the tension broke like an icicle from a warmed roof as they both began to laugh.

"You're cruel, Leah. You can't leave me in this condition."

She glanced at his very obvious *condition*. She bit one side of her lip and raised an eyebrow as she looked up at him.

"What do you expect me to do about it? Your daughter's home." She raised an eyebrow. "Or maybe you want me to throw pebbles at your window later tonight, and we can sneak out to neck in the peanut patch."

He groaned, pulling her into his arms once more and burying his face in her shoulder. With one last kiss, he put her away from him as the sound of the back door slamming reverberated down the hallway.

"We'll finish this," he promised, his husky whisper shivering over her skin. "Soon."

Six

Wade didn't think he'd ever seen Leah looking more beautiful. He could hardly believe she'd left her hair down. He hoped she'd done it for him, although looking like a goddess was reason enough for her to sweep the dark tresses to the side and clip them at her shoulder. Her hair flowed forward like rippling chocolate, contrasting with the white ruffles of her shirt.

He hadn't thought about what a tiny waist she had until now. With her shirt tucked into her denim skirt, her lush, hourglass figure was deliciously outlined and his mouth watered.

Actually, he hadn't thought about much else except tasting her, and he'd had very little sleep from the moment she'd left the night before. After he'd gotten his body under control, he'd joined Jonathan in the barn. He'd ignored the knowing look Jonathan had given him and had gone to work.

At two in the morning, long after Jonathan had headed home, Wade had taken his second shower of the evening—this one full cold. It hadn't helped. Whoever decided a cold shower would douse desire was an idiot.

After a few fitful hours of rest, he'd given up on sleep. With the party now in full swing, he was beginning to feel the lack of rest.

Leah had done a beautiful job, just as he'd known she would. The guests from both families were mingling nicely, the band was playing a variety of rhythms, and the refreshments were abundant. He'd heard the first real laugh from Myra Jo in months, and she was fairly glowing as she made the rounds on Pennington's arm.

"She's so beautiful."

Leah's voice came from his left. He looked down at her and breathed, "Beautiful."

He knew she'd heard because a blush stained the exposed portion of her throat a sweet pink.

She coughed delicately. It made him smile.

"You're mighty pretty yourself," she said in her best Texas twang, turning the tables on him.

He glanced at the moss green shirt with green suede yokes she'd bought him, the fabric a heavy but almost downy soft cotton. He hated to admit it, but with the bolo tie she'd picked, he did look pretty sharp.

"Thank you. I appreciate your help."

"You're welcome," she said with mock humility. He knew she was proud of her makeover. "And I'm glad everything is going so well. I hope you're pleased."

"I'm happier than a pig in a poke."

She gave him one of her exasperated glances, the one that warned him about putting on the redneck act.

He didn't care. He liked it when she looked at him, however she looked at him, whenever she looked at him.

"I'm proud of you, you know."

He drew back, startled. "Me? Why?"

"You didn't punch Penn's father out when he started politicking right in the middle of dinner."

"No, but I wanted to stuff one of those wet washrags the waiters handed out into his mouth."

Leah giggled. "I know. I did, too."

But in the end, a beautiful, cloud-free evening and the sprawling crowd helped keep Wade and Johnson Bradford apart.

"Would you like to dance?" Wade asked suddenly.

Leah looked regretful. "I wish I could, but I've got to go check on my crew and then make a round of the guests."

Unfortunately he knew she was right. Even he, who defied convention at a blink, couldn't ask her in one breath to do a job and in the next to neglect it. Especially for something as base as satisfying the desire coursing through his body.

Minimizing their physical contact was probably for the best, anyway. If he held her close and smelled the distinctive, pure womanly scent of her, he just might drag her to his bedroom and cause the scandal of the month.

Leah had started for the kitchen when the doorbell rang. She turned back around.

"I'll get it," he called to her, and hurried to answer an impatient second summons from the bell.

He opened the door to find Julie waiting, decked out in the gaudiest Texas chic and the biggest diamonds money could buy.

"Wade, darling, how nice of you to answer the door for me."

"Julie," he said, his face a mask. "I thought you weren't coming until the wedding itself."

Her face tightened and her eyes narrowed for a quick glare before she remembered herself and gave an airy laugh. "Don't be absurd, Wade. I can't miss my little girl's big evening."

He eyed her coldly, wondering what her real reason was for coming. No doubt one of Bradford's cronies in attendance tonight was on a zoning committee considering one of Julie's husband's properties, or some such nonsense. Which meant she was here to suck up to the legislators, and Myra Jo's party was merely an excuse so her bribes wouldn't be obvious.

"Are you going to stare at me all night, Wade, or are you going to let me in?"

Her words were as cool as her smile. He wanted to shut the door in her face, but relented and stepped away.

She walked by him and he couldn't stop himself from asking, "No Ratford with you tonight, Julie?"

She gave him an arch look. "It's Redford, Wade, but you know that. And he's too busy right now with a new deal he's putting together. He'll be with me at the wedding, however."

"I'm overjoyed to hear it."

Julie's smile was smug as she made a turn she'd learned in private modeling lessons—she'd mentioned them to Myra Jo enough times—and headed out to the patio with a few queenly nods to people she knew. Her target was obviously the over-fifty and overweight set near the dancing area.

Wade went outside, grabbing a beer as he took a post by the lawn canopy, which afforded him the best view of the crowd. A few folks stopped to chat, but mostly he was alone with his thoughts. He watched Julie working the crowd and decided she should be the lieutenant governor, not the tall man she was schmoozing with.

"Hey, what's the matter?"

Wade closed his eyes. Just the sound of Leah's voice was enough to make him feel things would be all right.

"See the well-kept blonde with the lieutenant governor?"

Leah followed the direction he indicated with his beer bottle.

"She's Myra Jo's mother."

"I thought she wasn't coming until the wedding."

"I guess that's what we both get for thinking. She's not really here to see Myra Jo. It's been nearly forty-five minutes, and she hasn't let one particular crony of Bradford's out of her clutches. I wonder who she's bribing and what for."

"Ah, there's the cynical Wade I've come to know and love."

He managed a half smile and a quarter chuckle. "I guess I'm not being incredibly mature at the moment, am I?"

"No, but you're being charmingly protective of your little girl."

"Thanks," he said, releasing a pent-up breath. "It's nice to feel I don't have to explain myself to you."

Their conversation stopped as Myra Jo and Penn came from the pool area and Julie saw them. She put on a greeting scene worthy of an award. Wade was sure the audience believed Julie's touching, and loud, avowal of how much she'd missed her baby, but he could tell Leah was noting Myra Jo's strained features.

"I'm so sorry," Leah said quietly, her eyes sad.

"Me, too. At one time I thought Julie would take the risk of loving Myra Jo, but I think being close to someone scared Julie too much. She became even more closed."

Leah gave him an appraising glance. "That's very insightful."

He smiled down at her. "For a redneck or for a man?"

She returned a cheeky grin. "Both."

He watched Myra Jo for a moment. He ached from seeing her glowing happiness fade to an anxious frown. He wanted to intervene, but Myra Jo seemed to be holding her own. She would merely resent him for butting in, anyway. He was finding letting go harder than his worst imagining.

"Come on," he said, taking Leah's arm. "Let's go for a walk. I'll help you with monitor duty."

He actually found he enjoyed the slow tour as they headed inside. Leah's beautiful smile and easy personality made each short stop at this or that cluster of people pleasant. In between groups she sent her staff to attend to the small details he'd never noticed. Like most folks, he had guessed peanut bowls magically refilled themselves and spilled popcorn took itself to the vacuum cleaner.

As he'd expected, things were livelier when they returned outside. The staff assigned to the lawn area and poolside were hopping, but Leah said it was a promising sign, not a concern. Laughter rang out freely among the mixed groups, and there were lots of smiling faces to be seen. He decided to take a chance on corrupting her sense of duty for a few minutes.

Leading her away from the noise, he headed toward the back paddock. Myra Jo's horse didn't like strangers, so knowing folks would visit the front paddock and the barn, they'd put Lightning Two out of the range of any sightseers.

Her smile told him she knew what he was doing, but as she made no move to stop him, he pressed his luck. He walked to the back corner, under the canopy of a pecan tree that had survived all that nature and man had thrown its way. In the heat of the day, the horses vied for the generous shade thrown by its long limbs, and tonight its canopy of leaves created a quiet island of darkness. The sounds of the party were faint in the soft swish of the branches being tossed by the summer winds.

"She's magnificent," Leah said, eyeing the far end of the paddock.

Lightning Two stood with her head down, poking her nose through the slats of the fence to pull grass from the other side. The brilliant moon, not quite full, but powerfully radiant, cast the horse's white coat into an almost eerie relief.

"That horse is one hundred percent Myra Jo's, just as her mother, White Lightning, was. Lightning Two will let me brush her down and exercise her, but she won't tolerate much else."

"Is that unusual?"

"Not really. Horses are as individual as people, and how they're socialized makes a difference. I bought White Lightning as a filly for Myra Jo when they were both just about to turn four. Lightning Two came later, and you'd think both horses had mind links with her or something. If you wanted to find Myra Jo when she was upset, all you had to do was find her horse."

Leah nodded absently. "I always wanted a place to hide when I was younger, but with six siblings, I never got the chance. Even if I'd had a place, I would never have managed to be alone."

Wade placed a comforting arm around her shoulders. Wrapping her arms around his waist, she rested her head on the broad expanse of his chest, stealing a moment of pure peacefulness as the wind fought with Wade's fingers for rights to her hair. Her ear was filled with the sound of his strong heartbeat.

Knowing they'd already stolen too much time, Leah reluctantly stepped away. They kept an arm around each other as they walked out of the shelter of the tree. When he stopped her before they passed the gate, yet remained hidden by the barn, she felt the thrill of anticipation. At least she was going to get one kiss tonight.

She moved willingly into his embrace, sighing as he bent

and nuzzled underneath her ear. "This isn't a good idea, you know," she said in opposition to her actions.

"I think it's a great idea," he answered against her throat.

"We're going to get into trouble."

"Mmm, I certainly hope so."

"Wade, you're not listening to me."

"You're right. I'm too busy smelling you."

He moved his head to take the lobe of her ear gently in his teeth. "You're enchanting."

Leah moaned softly as he traced the side of her neck with the tip of his nose. Nudging her face toward his, Wade covered her waiting lips. His kiss was as liquid and intoxicating as the moonlight, and his arms around her felt just as heavenly. He made her feel as though she filled his every thought, and any moment away from her was torture—and all with just his tantalizing lips.

Myra Jo's voice shattered the moment.

"Daddy! What are you doing?"

She and Wade jumped apart like guilty teenagers, and Leah immediately noticed the moonlight glinting off Myra Jo's tear-filled eyes.

Wade moved toward her. "Honey, what's wrong?"

Myra Jo stepped back. "Don't touch me. Don't any of you touch me."

Her voice broke as she fumbled with the gate, then ran toward her horse. Lightning Two gave a startled toss of her head but upon recognizing her mistress, immediately trotted forward.

Leah's heart wrenched as she saw Myra Jo latch her arms around the horse's neck and cry into the frosty white coat.

Wade followed, taking Leah's hand and pulling her with him.

He let her go when they had nearly reached the horse. Leah wanted to cry, too, when Myra Jo refused the comfort of her father's arms. Wade wouldn't back away, though, making Leah proud of him. She knew tears were hard on John Wayne types, but Wade waited until Myra Jo's crying abated, then simply handed her a white handkerchief he'd pulled from his back pocket.

After blowing her nose, Myra Jo moved back, and the most inept observer could have seen her gearing up to have her say.

"Go ahead, sweetheart. Let me have it."

"Don't try to make me laugh, Daddy. I'm really upset."

"I know. I promise I won't tease. Tell me what's wrong."

"It's a lot of things, but I just can't take it anymore. I was doing okay until Julie started talking like we're so close you couldn't put a toothpick between us, going on and on about how excited Redford is about having such a close connection to the capitol now, and then Mr. Bradford started in on what a wonderful addition I am to the family and how beautiful we'll all look standing behind the podium when he makes his acceptance speech."

She paced a length and turned on Wade.

"And you, Daddy, you're the worst of all. At least Julie and Mr. Bradford are so transparent you could use them for a window. But you have gone on and on for a year now about how miserable I'm going to be with the Bradfords, when what you're really worried about is Mr. Bradford using me to blackmail you into supporting some plan of his."

"Oh, baby, that's not—"

"And then, to top it off, I finally find the perfect person to coordinate my wedding, and you make a move on her!"

Tears started slowly rolling down her cheeks again, and Leah thought Wade looked as though his heart were breaking.

"We didn't hire Leah for you, Daddy," she said in a tear-strangled voice, "we hired her for me. Me, damn it, and I'm not going to let you spoil my wedding because you're too stubborn to see my love for Penn. And he loves me, Daddy. Seduce Leah, I don't care. Turn her to your side. But you're not stopping my wedding, if I have to do it all myself.''

"Myra Jo, I—''

She began walking toward the gate. "No. No more words tonight. Just leave me alone.''

Leah waited until he had watched Myra Jo walk out of sight before moving close to him. "Come on. Let's head back.''

He didn't seem to hear her.

"God, Leah, what am I going to do?''

Leah knew what she wanted to do. This was one of those rare circumstances when she felt inclined to pry into someone's personal business. It was obvious that no matter what Wade said, Myra Jo couldn't listen, and any attempt on his part to approach first would only make things worse.

"You can't do anything for the moment. We're going back to the party where you will continue being the charming host, and I'll talk to Myra Jo later and reassure her. Since she sees me as the seducee instead of the seducer, she might consider me less of a threat, which is exactly what I plan to be.''

Wade looked hopeful for a brief second before shaking his head. "Thank you, but no. I'll handle this my way.''

She acquiesced reluctantly, returning to the party without additional comment. She saw him take Myra Jo aside some time later, and while Leah didn't witness the hugging reconciliation she'd hoped for, it appeared they'd come to some sort of resolution. Myra Jo and her father seemed less tense as they bid good-night to the many guests.

Myra Jo left with Penn, telling her father she wouldn't be home. Leah was pleased to see he took the news with more grace than he had at the boutique, but she knew it still bothered him.

Bless his old-fashioned heart. He thought women should be nurtured and protected. This women's lib stuff was tolerable—for other men's daughters.

The house seemed to reverberate with silence as they took down the equipment, tables, and decorations. Wade worked tirelessly, turning on the stereo to cover the quiet. She didn't try to stop him as he was obviously too antsy to sit still, and he'd never go to bed with the crew still there. The familiar oldies coming from the speakers provided a nice background as they tackled their tasks.

Leah was sure he was thinking about Myra Jo until she caught him watching her. Clearly, his thoughts were not on his daughter, or her pending nuptials. Leah finally realized she was affording him quite a view when she leaned forward to pick up something and the vee of her shirt would gape. Nothing graphic, just enough to make a man of his moral character fight his baser instincts. She was amused to see him look, then flush and force his attention away.

Once she was aware, of course, she was careful to be more modest. She still thought he was charming and sweet. Most men would have ogled.

When she met his steady gaze, his hunger unmasked, her hands fluttered to a stop. She was captured by the passion that turned his eyes the gray of a stormy sky and held a promise just as exciting, just as enthralling. Just as dangerous.

"Send your crew home, Leah."

Seven

She didn't pretend to misunderstand. She'd never been one for games, and she wasn't playing one now, even if she was short of breath. Her skin tingled as he continued to hold her with just the power of his eyes.

"Send your crew home, Leah."

His repeated command broke her trance. With a modicum of control, she thought about what he was asking without asking. Yet even as she headed toward the kitchen, she knew what her answer would be. Some things were inevitable, and from their first evening together on Town Lake, a part of her soul had known this moment would eventually come.

The crew had already cleared the patio, dining room and kitchen. Her practical side said she and Wade could handle the rest of the cleanup by themselves...tomorrow. Her staff was more than willing to call it quits early, taking the news with bright smiles and quick good-nights before she changed her mind.

Mere seconds had passed before Wade came up behind her, shutting the door after the last server and locking it with a click. He never took his eyes from her as he grasped her hand and walked into the huge den still bearing the remains of the party.

Wade had turned off the lights, but the tapers still flickered on the mantel. The gentle whirring of the ceiling fan made the candlelight waver and wafted the gentle scent of mulberry throughout the room. He had turned down the stereo, but the sounds of the soft music filled the quiet.

Leah let him lead her to the center of the room, but instead of the kiss she was expecting, he tucked her head under his chin and began dancing with her to the romantic sound of strings and brass. She didn't realize how tense she was until the warmth of him seeped deeply into her. The gentle sway of their bodies and the wholly masculine scent of him finally reached past the part of her brain still checking lists, and her muscles let go.

"Finally," he whispered into her hair, placing a kiss against her brow.

"Finally, what?"

"You're finally here."

"Silly man. I've been here all day."

"No, you've been on the job all day. Now you're finally with me."

Leah didn't argue when he snuggled her closer. She didn't want to think about how his words disconcerted her. She didn't want to consider this was the first time she'd ever been in a man's arms and felt totally at peace.

She forced her muscles to stay relaxed as her thoughts began to whirl. More than Wade being wrong for her because of her profession and life-style, he was pure danger to her control. There was no doubt she wanted to make love with him, but she told herself she'd better be careful.

Now was the time to get out if she didn't think she could handle what came next.

She wondered why she was even debating with herself. She had already made her decision, and she would keep her mind clear and her heart protected. She would enjoy this night and cherish it forever, but she would never lose the innermost part of herself. After all, she never had before.

"Hey, where'd you go?"

She snuggled into the hollow of his neck again. "Nowhere," she fibbed, once more feeling she had mastered the moment.

Another kiss against her brow drove everything from her mind but the sensation of being wrapped in the arms of the sexiest cowboy on the planet. She moved her hands up his neck to comb her fingernails through his short, soft hair— hair the same color as the coarser curls tickling her nose through the vee in his shirt.

His body was a tailor's nightmare, but a woman's dream. Broad shoulders braced her arms, and the muscular chest supporting her head narrowed sharply to lean hips. The taut stomach and long legs she was deliciously anticipating seeing unclothed pressed intimately against hers as he turned her in time with the music.

She wondered why she hadn't begun to feel self-conscious about her own not-so-toned-and-tanned physique, but yet another brush of his soft, warm lips against her temple stalled any cataloging of her shortcomings. All she could do was live in the sensations of this second in time. She'd dreamed about experiencing such a moment—a moment in which she felt as though nothing existed but herself and the man who held her as if he would die if he had to let her go.

Her pulse quickened as he unclasped her hair clip and tossed it toward the coffee table.

"Like liquid silk." He sighed, running his fingers from her nape to the ends of her hair, then cupping her head and lifting her face to his.

The moment their lips met, a fire ignited. Gone were the gentle touches, the provocative brush of bodies. In place was an animal hunger, a thirst too long denied, demanding to be assuaged.

His lips were hard against hers, his tongue an erotic invasion. Every nerve in her body came alive at once, making her ache as he pulled her blouse from her skirt and slipped the buttons from their closures, revealing her breasts to his hungry gaze. She could hardly stand, clutching him as he removed the rest of her clothes and gently pressed her down on the sofa. She whimpered as he moved back to strip off his own clothes.

Never had she felt this wanton, never had she needed a man to press into her and claim her body as she did now. When his mouth closed over her aching breast, she arched against him with a cry, burying her fingers in his hair and pulling him even closer.

His left hand held her breast as he lavished his attention on the aching peak. His right hand sent shock waves through her. He stroked down her hips in a trail of fire, only to draw the blaze up the inside of her thigh until his fingers grazed the hot, moist center of her.

He claimed her mouth in a kiss that sent her senses spinning. His demanding invasion aroused her to a level she had never known, leaving her panting in a maelstrom of need, at the mercy of his gentle torture.

She barely contained a scream as his mouth followed the trail of his hands. She wanted to tell him to stop, that she was embarrassed, but when his tongue began to tease the sensitive nub hidden in her velvet folds, she couldn't think. She couldn't speak. All she could do was toss her head as wave after wave of pleasure crashed over her and left her gasping his name.

He was relentless, bringing her to peak after peak of pleasure until she was sure she would die from the glory of it.

But she didn't. Instead, she slowly returned to earth as he covered her body with soft kisses until she could finally breathe again. She moved her chin when he nuzzled into her neck and welcomed his weight on top of her. She opened to him, taking him between her waiting thighs, anxious to feel him within her.

He lifted his head to look into her eyes as he slowly sank himself into her depth. They both gasped at the exquisite sensation. He waited, just waited, for an eternity, and then began to move in a primal rhythm, quickly rebuilding the fire within her to its former inferno.

He slipped his arms around her as the demands of his desire took over. His body thrust against hers, and she urged him on, begging him to move higher, faster. With her hands on his hips and her legs wrapped around his, she demanded he go with her to that place of exquisite release.

Her name burst from his lips as he climaxed, her own cry of joy reverberating against the paneled walls.

His breathing was harsh and ragged as he rested his head on her shoulder. She held him close, glorying in the feel of his weight against her.

"You are…so…passionate," he whispered in her ear, stroking her shoulder and collarbone with shaking fingers, "so responsive."

Much too soon he lifted his head to kiss her. With an embarrassed laugh he said, "I'm sorry. I'm crushing you."

Moving his weight off her, he stretched out on his back on the floor beside her, still trying to catch his breath. Even though he held her hand, kissing her palm and pressing it against his beating heart, a cold wash of reality hit her.

She was terrified. She wanted to call him back to her, to beg him to take her in his arms again, to keep this awful feeling away. If he had stayed with her, if they could have snuggled together, maybe she could have stayed warm, but with each second her body was turning to stone.

"No," she whispered, a tear slipping down her cheek. "Not yet. Let me have this moment, just this once, help me let go."

But her prayer wasn't granted. She yanked her hand from his to search frantically for something to cover herself with. The first thing she found was his shirt and she shrugged it on, clutching the two sides together with bloodless fingers.

"Leah! What—" Wade sat up, startled, as she rushed past.

Even spent from passion, he was quicker than she imagined, catching her in the hallway and spinning her to face him. She could only imagine what she looked like, her hair a wild mess around her and dressed in his shirt.

"Leah, what's wrong?"

His face was anxious, but Leah assured herself the hurt she thought she saw was only a trick of the dim hallway.

"Please let me go," she managed to say past her constricted throat.

"Not until you tell me what's wrong."

"Wade, please—"

Her voice was anguished, but instead of complying with her wishes, he pulled her against him, wrapping one arm around her back and cradling her head against his shoulder with the other.

"Darling, tell me what happened. What did I do? Whatever it is, I'm so sorry."

Mortified, she felt tears stream down her face and onto his chest. As he held her so tenderly, with such care, she could not control the sobs taking over.

She had no idea how long they stood there before the

tremors finally abated. He nudged her face up with his knuckle to wipe her tears away with the pads of his thumbs.

"Can you tell me now?"

She shook her head. "No, Wade, I—"

He turned her around and pushed her gently toward the bathroom. "Splash some cold water on your face. I'll get us something to drink. Then we'll talk."

Her hands were shaking so hard she could barely close the door behind her. She sat down on the side of the tub, the cold porcelain biting at her bare thighs. She waited for berating thoughts to assail her, but it seemed as if her brain had simply shut down. Nothing came, except her need to brush her hair and clean the smudged makeup from her face.

She didn't look at her reflection as she wiped her eyes with a soft washcloth. She didn't need a mirror to tell her her expression would be lost, her complexion ashen, her eyes haunted.

She picked up the big silver brush lying on the counter next to a hand mirror. She didn't care if it was for decoration. She wouldn't have cared if it had been Myra Jo's. She had to get the wanton disarray away from her face before she screamed. She wielded the heavy brush through her long hair with vicious strokes, not stopping until each strand was smooth again. With surprisingly deft fingers, considering their former trembling, she wove an even braid, but knew the silky strands would never stay without her clip. Again, she didn't care. For now she felt she had a semblance of order.

She cast a longing glance at the bathroom window. Not only would she be an idiot to sneak out in her near naked condition, but she could hardly walk home. Her purse and keys were in Wade's office, and he was between her and her means of escape.

With a ragged but somewhat fortifying breath, she

smoothed the rumpled shirt over her hips and tried to gather some dignity around her as she returned to the den. He was sitting on the sofa, obviously waiting for her, two glasses of chilled wine in his hands.

She stood in the archway, wanting to grab the clothes he had thoughtfully folded for her, except they were on the cushion next to him. She couldn't bring herself to move any closer to his half-clad body.

Even in her near numb state, her mind betrayed her by cataloguing his bare, muscled chest, the zipped but unsnapped jeans hugging his lean hips and strong legs, and his bare feet. To stand there thinking his bare feet were sexy at a moment like this only proved her insanity.

"Um...could you hand me my clothes, please? I'd like to get dressed before we...um...talk."

"No."

She stared at him for a moment, quite sure she had heard him wrong. "What?"

"I said no. If I give you these clothes, you'll get all prim and businesslike, and then I'll never get the truth from you. You use your clothes and hair like armor—your clothes all professional and neat, and your hair tortured and under control."

His words were somehow fortifying, giving her the strength to pull back her shoulders and shoot him a quelling glare. "I don't think I've ever been called a liar in such a backhanded fashion before."

Wade rubbed his face with his hands before trying again. "I didn't mean it that way. I just meant you're already so far away from me I couldn't reach you with the space shuttle. The last thing I need is to add a brick wall."

She didn't try to figure out his mangled analogy because she knew what he meant. She didn't like it, but she knew.

Hanging on to the tattered remains of her dignity, Leah smoothed the long tails of his shirt under her as she carefully took a seat in an armchair across from him. She felt her hair slip from the impromptu braid and cascade over her shoulder of its own volition just as she clasped her hands in her lap.

"You know," he said, his voice containing the husky timbre that had been her undoing some moments ago, "you look sexy as hell sitting there with nothing on but my shirt and that glorious hair of yours."

She couldn't think of a suitable reply, not with her mind occupied with her body's response to him. How could that possibly be happening? She was in the most awkward position she'd ever been in, yet her pulse was starting to race, and her body was going all hot and moist.

She had to get out of there.

"Wade, I know you want to talk, but I just can't. I'm sorry, I was going to try, but you have to let me go."

She clenched her hands together so tightly her knuckles turned white as she struggled to control the tears that threatened behind her eyelids. She'd already made a blubbering fool of herself once tonight; she didn't care for a repeat performance.

Glancing up, she met his eyes and felt a flood of relief. She could tell he wasn't unmoved by her distress, and in fact, he was rising to hand her clothes to her.

"Just tell me one thing," he said as she clutched her skirt and shirt to her chest. "Tell me what I did wrong."

One traitorous tear slipped past her guard as she tried to take some deep breaths. She finally looked up and met his eyes.

"Oh, Wade, you didn't do anything wrong. It was... unbelievable."

"Then why are you sitting here like I'm about to attack you, for God's sake," he growled out, despite his obvious attempt to control his temper.

She stood and edged away from him, not answering until

she was almost in the hallway again. "Because I lost control."

She could tell he didn't understand. Maybe the concept was too female for a man to grasp.

"Oh, Wade, don't you see? There's nothing you couldn't have asked of me tonight that I wouldn't have done. I would have played any game, done anything you wanted, without one thought to the consequence to my soul. No one's ever done that to me. And no one ever will again."

Feeling like a coward, she turned and hurried down the hall to the bathroom again, dressing in record time. She still had no way to secure her hair, but at least she was covered, and for the first time in hours, she took a full breath.

He had her purse and shoes waiting for her when she made the final trip into the den. She slipped on her pumps and found her keys while advancing toward her escape out the back door. He let her get almost the whole way through the kitchen before he grasped her elbow. She jumped, not from fear, but from the electric jolt his mere touch sent through her.

"We have to talk about this, you know."

She fiddled with her purse strap and gave an ambiguous movement of her head.

"I'll send my crew back out tomorrow morning to finish."

"Don't worry about it. I can take care of what's left."

"No, really—"

"Leah, let it go. I'll call you tomorrow, but don't worry about the house."

She nodded stiffly and headed for her car, grateful to the night air for cooling her flushed skin.

She made it a whole six miles before she had to turn off the highway and sob against the steering wheel.

* * *

Wade turned off the lights as he traveled to his bedroom. He stripped off his jeans and slipped between the cool sheets, still totally bewildered. Of course she'd lost control! She'd gone out-of-her-mind out of control, tossing and moaning like a wild woman. That was what great sex was all about.

He didn't have to be a rocket scientist to figure out Leah had power issues, but mind-blowing orgasms certainly shouldn't have sent her off the deep end. The joy he'd gotten from her passionate response to him, along with no small stroke to his ego, were destroyed by the stark terror he'd seen in her eyes when the loving had ended.

He might not be Don Juan, but he felt he knew enough about good sex to satisfy both his partner and himself without experiencing the reaction he'd gotten tonight.

His ego wasn't bothering him, though. What hurt, deep in his heart, was Leah's reaction. He could see it had very little to do with sex, and everything to do with her foundation being shaken. He could think of no other explanation for the haunted, cornered look he'd seen on her face.

One thing was for sure: he wasn't going to let her run away or avoid him. He was going to get to the bottom of this little mystery, whether Leah liked it or not.

Eight

Leah carried on as usual, refusing to let anyone see how close she was to tears. It was safer, much safer, to retreat into the familiar routine of a long, hard day of work than face the memory of last evening. Even though her conscience berated her, she had her assistant hold all calls, and buried herself in a mountain of paperwork.

She wasn't aware of time passing. When her assistant asked if she wanted some lunch, Leah's stomach recoiled. Accepting a cold drink instead, she went right back to her tasks and ignored the rising number of messages in her holder.

When the shop was nearly silent and the sun had moved from one set of windows to the other, she knew the time had to be around six, but she was in the groove and had no intention of quitting. If she kept up this pace, she could be caught up by midnight or so, and then she might be exhausted enough to sleep.

The door opened, and Rhonda stuck her head in.

"Hey, you. When are you coming out of hiding?"

"Tomorrow. I'm actually getting caught up," she added brightly, waving toward the stack of folders in her Out box.

"Impressive, even for a workaholic like you."

Leah shrugged and finished a note on the file in front of her. She was hoping Rhonda would take the hint and go away, but when she looked up again, Rhonda had entered, closed the door behind her and was sitting impatiently across from her.

"Are you going to tell me or not?"

"Tell—"

"And don't play innocent. Something happened last night, and you're a wreck. So give."

"It's nothing I can't handle. I just need some time."

"You had sex with him, didn't you?"

"Just because I'm a little uptight today doesn't mean—"

"Yep. Sex. No doubt about it."

Leah had to smile in spite of her knotted muscles and aching head. "Are you a mind reader, or just psychic?"

"Neither. A blind man could guess from the look on your face." Rhonda sat back and scrunched down in the chair, folding her arms over her stomach. "I believe this is the part where you tell me it was no big deal and won't happen again."

Leah searched under a stack of folders. "I think I've lost my *Discussing Your Personal Sex Life with Your Friends* manual. Can I borrow your copy?"

Rhonda rolled her eyes. "Why are you being so difficult? Wade's absolutely gorgeous. Runs in the Mackey family. I know."

Leah looked up sharply. "What does that mean?"

Rhonda studied one perfectly manicured nail. "I knew Jonathan in high school. We were 'just friends.'"

"Uh-oh. Sounds like an unrequited crush to me. Why didn't you tell me this before?"

"No need. I didn't expect to see Jonathan, even at the wedding, since I'll be in the background the whole time, but I thought maybe you'd feel better if I confessed to knowing the sexual power of any male named Mackey."

Leah shifted in her seat. "It's not like I planned this."

"Do we ever? Isn't there a rule somewhere that the guys who are perfect for us don't merit a second glance, but the ones we should stay a mile away from get us every time?"

Leah laughed. "Yeah, and Wade Mackey scared the hell out of me last night."

"I can't imagine sex with such a gorgeous guy could be bad."

"Oh, the sex was great. Too great, in fact."

Rhonda frowned. "There's no such thing as too great sex."

"For me there is. I lost total control last night, Rhonda."

Rhonda sat forward and her face lost all hint of teasing. "Ah. I understand. Are you okay?"

"No, as a matter of fact. I don't know what to do. I have to finish this wedding, and not just because I need to repair my professional reputation."

"You should have left sex for after the wedding."

"Thanks, but your advice is a tad late."

"So what are you going to do?"

"I don't know, but I'll figure something out. It's a darn good thing I have two weeks until I have to face him at the rehearsal dinner. Maybe I can think of a plan by then."

The bell on the front door chimed and Rhonda stood. "Sounds like the last one out forgot to lock the door. I'll handle it."

"Thanks, my friend. I'll be back to normal tomorrow, I promise, and I'll shoulder my full share."

"You do more than your share now. Just get some rest."

Rhonda left, only to return a moment later. "Um, Leah? You know those two weeks you were counting on?"

Leah nodded, confused. "Yeah? What about—"

Rhonda moved aside and opened the door its full width. At her shoulder stood Leah's nemesis himself.

"I'll see you tomorrow." Rhonda moved away.

"Rhonda, wait!"

"Have a nice chat, you two."

Traitor, Leah sent to her retreating friend.

"You didn't return my calls."

Leah folded her hands together. "You don't go in for chitchat much, do you, Wade?"

"I've been trying to reach you all day."

"I didn't answer because I haven't checked my messages yet. I had too much work today, so I had all my calls held."

"You knew I would try to reach you."

"Did you bring thumbscrews with you, or are you just going to browbeat me?"

"I'm not kidding, Leah."

His expression was so contained, Leah knew he was furious—furious enough to drive all the way into Austin to talk to her. She tried to bolster the incredibly scared part of her that was terrified at the thought of facing him.

"You're here now, so what can I do for you?"

Wade moved a step forward and planted his hands on her desk with a hard slap.

With his face mere inches from hers, he said, "Talk to me."

She almost faltered, but caught herself just in time. Meeting him stare for stare, she answered, "I am talking to you, but if you don't get out of my face, I'm going to punch you."

He didn't move an inch. "Anything would be better than this ice princess act."

She actually smiled. "It's ice queen, and I've been called

that by men bigger than you, Wade Mackey. I didn't give in to them, and I won't to you.''

Actually, she'd lied. The men who had called her frigid had never been as tall and as rugged as he was, but she hardly felt inclined to bring up such details at the moment.

Wade jerked away from her desk and paced an angry circle around her chairs and back beside her desk.

''Leah—''

The phone rang and she grabbed it. ''Leah Houston.''

She watched Wade pace again and then sit. She listened to her caller and umm-hmmed and I see'd at the appropriate moments. She ended the call with, ''Congratulations, Brandt. I hope you'll be happy.''

When she hung up, she looked at Wade, reclasping her hands.

He looked at her curiously, then at the telephone and back again.

She sighed. ''Though no business of yours, the caller was my boyfriend calling to tell me he's getting married. Ex-boyfriend now, I guess. Was there anything else we needed to finish before you leave so I can get back to work?''

''You're acting awfully nonchalant.''

''Oh, we've hardly seen each other in the past six months, so I'm not exactly surprised.''

''I'm not talking about your stupid boyfriend.''

''He was brilliant, actually. Is brilliant. Oh, hell, you know what I mean. He's going to own Wall Street some day.''

''I don't give a damn about Brandt,'' Wade said through his teeth. ''Stop it, Leah.''

''Yeah, I irritated the bejeebers out of Brandt, too,'' Leah said, rearranging her stapler and Rolodex. ''But it worked, because I'd—''

Wade pulled her out of her chair and into his arms in one smooth motion. His mouth was punishingly hard for a

moment before his lips turned seeking, coaxing, irresistibly
tempting. If he was trying to communicate his needs to her
without words, he was doing a good job of it. Her whole
body had responded the instant his hands had touched her
arms. Just as she'd known she would. Just as she'd dreaded.
Just as she'd hoped.

Wade let her go and scowled. "Damn you, woman,
you're making me nuts!"

She sat down, grateful her shaky legs didn't have to hold
her. "I think you were already nuts when you walked in
here."

"You're right. I haven't had any sleep in two days, and
I'm a little on the edge. Talk to me, Leah!"

She relented a bit. "Wade, I'm sorry you're out of sorts,
but I'm not ready to talk—to you or Rhonda or anyone
else. If I so much as think about you, I'm going to splinter
into a thousand little pieces, and I'm not ready to do that.
So if you don't mind, go home, take a sleeping pill and
leave me be."

He looked at her for a long, long time. She knew she
could get lost in those gray depths, *had* gotten lost in them,
and the nearly overwhelming urge to do it again made her
tremble. How easily she could lose herself in a strength
like his. It called to the side of her that was tired of being
strong, tired of being dependable, tired of being responsible. She was very aware of the traitorous voice whispering
she could let go with Wade; but she knew better. She could
not abdicate who she was, even for a man as sexy, as handsome, as wonderful as he.

In his inimitable style, Wade stood up and held out his
hand to her. "Come on, I'm taking you home."

"What?"

"I'm taking—"

"I heard you. I guess what I meant was no."

"You look as tired as I feel. I'm not going to let you drive in this condition."

She stared at him, shaking her head. "You're not going to *let* me? This may come as a shock to you, but you have no authority over me."

They faced off over her desk, and Leah was amazed when Wade dropped his eyes first. Glad, but amazed.

"Look, Wade, in a way I understand what you're going through. You're used to being the boss, the head of the family, the owner of a prosperous business. Except for the family thing, I'm used to the same thing, and neither of us takes orders well."

He gave a short nod. "Truce then. *May* I drive you home?"

"I don't need—"

"Leah, please, I'm asking you to humor me. I have no fuse left, and the only way I'm going to be able to let this drop and get some sleep is if I'm sure you're home safe."

She bent her head. The second wind she had anticipated sustaining her for several more hours was gone, leaving her drained. A look at Wade showed he was equally exhausted, but she didn't have the heart to argue with him anymore.

"Okay, you win. Let's go."

"Thank you. I'll drop you off and then head over to a friend's house to crash."

"Where does your friend live?"

"Buda."

Staying silent during the short drive to her house proved a challenge. She could tell Wade was staying awake by sheer will, and her conscience would not allow her to let him drive the thirty-five to forty minutes from her house to his friend's. No matter how much fire she was playing with, she just couldn't.

When he pulled to a stop, she put a hand on his arm. "Wade, come up with me."

"No, but thanks. If I stop now, I'll never make it."

"You asked me for a favor, now I'm asking you. Please come in for a while."

Weary as he was, a spark of desire glowed in his eyes. "Leah, you need to understand. If I get some rest and wake up in the same room as you, I'm going to make love to you."

"Then we won't sleep in the same room. Problem solved."

He pulled into her reserved parking space and hesitated before he turned off the engine.

"We'll see. Just don't say I didn't warn you."

Fatigue made them both look slightly drunk as they walked up the stone path. If she hadn't been so tired, she'd probably have laughed herself into hiccups. As it was, she opened her door and ushered Wade in to lock them safely inside.

Safely? Well, a version of the word, anyway.

Wade was unsteady as he leaned against her counter. "Leah, I'm sorry I've pushed so hard today. I'll just rest for a minute and then I'll head out. I promise."

She led him to the sofa during his speech, and he sank into the comfortable cushions with a sigh. She swore no living soul would know she helped him take his boots off, hoping he wouldn't remember, either, when morning came. She rescued his hat from the back of the sofa and put it on the table. Before she could turn around to check, he'd stretched out and was snoring softly.

The only reason he even fitted on her couch was because she had ordered an extra-long design. She'd loved the thing when she'd placed her order, but had grown to dislike it as being out of balance with the rest of her decor. Now she was glad she hadn't had time to look for a replacement.

With a smile, she went to the linen closet and grabbed an extra pillow and light blanket. The air-conditioning and the ceiling fans kept her place comfortably cool, and she didn't want him to get chilled. At least, that was what she told herself as she carefully covered him and lifted his head to place the pillow beneath the short, silken strands of hair she accidentally ran her fingers through as she set his head back down.

She was halfway down the hall when she heard him mumble, and she stopped. She thought she heard the word *love* and her name in the same sentence. Shaking her head, she walked back to her room, obviously past the point of coherent thought if she was making up such nonsense. She glanced at the clock, hardly able to believe it was only seven-thirty. She yawned and decided she'd beat Wade at his own game. All she needed was a good nap, too, and she'd be up before him to ensure nothing got out of hand. Knowing she'd never sleep in her suit, she took it off and slipped on a robe, tying the belt securely at her waist. She stretched out on top of her comforter with a grateful sigh.

Wade awoke in the early hours of the morning. He oriented himself and realized he was lying on a bed in his jeans and socks, with Leah snuggled against him with her head on his bare shoulder. He ran his fingers lightly down the back of her robe, being careful not to disturb her, but the scent of her in his nostrils was too compelling to ignore.

He had a vague memory of falling asleep on her couch, so how had he ended up shirtless and in her bed? He had no recollection of moving, much less pulling Leah to him in this most satisfying of positions. Well, satisfying for the moment, anyway.

He felt a tiny bit of guilt about breaking his promise, but considering that he hadn't deliberately moved from the couch to her bed and how comfortably she was sleeping, it didn't seem right to wake her up and leave at—

He stretched his neck over Leah's shoulder to see her nightstand.

Three o'clock in the morning.

The only logical thing to do was snuggle down with her and let the morning take its course.

Nearly eight hours of sleep had left him wide awake, despite the early hour. He didn't mind, though, not with an exquisite female body pressed against him, making sleepy, murmuring noises against his shoulder. A feeling of being complete, even if illusory, was welcome for whatever time he could enjoy it.

The faint glow from a night-light gave just enough illumination for him to see her beautiful face, soft and peaceful in sleep. No tension marred the perfection of her skin. And, of course, her scent, so rich and warm and utterly sexy, was arousing him to the core of his being.

He tried to steer his thoughts away from their increasingly erotic path, which would only lead to trouble. Leah needed him to be gentle and to listen when she was ready to talk. If he left his thoughts unchecked, he was afraid he'd do very little listening and a whole lot of seducing.

He told himself to use the cool darkness as a chance to think. Sometimes he thought too much, or so he'd been accused, but it was nice to have an opportunity to muse at his leisure.

There was no doubt he could muse about Leah all day. In fact, he found himself musing much too often. Once, he'd been grooming Thunder, standing in the barn with Thunder's hoof in one hand, a pick in the other, and it had taken a thorough nudging from Thunder's strong nose to get him out of a Leah-induced trance and get on with his work. Wade was just glad his horse had chosen to nudge instead of bite.

Bite. What a good idea! Just a little one, a tiny nip, right on the curve of her shoulder, and then a few on her collarbone, then on to the hot, full swell of her breast.

Wade closed his eyes and took a slow, deep breath. He knew he had to stop, but it was asking too much of a man to lie on a comfortable bed with the woman of his dreams in his arms, half-naked, sexy in sleep. Then to expect the man to think logically and coolly, without wanting to turn her over and bury himself inside her, was monumentally unfair. Not when he knew just how passionate she was, how delicious, how perfectly suited to him in rhythm and intensity and response.

Leah stirred against his shoulder. With a deep sigh and a moan, she opened her eyes. "Hi," she said in a breathy voice. "I thought you were sleeping on the couch."

"I was. I swear, I don't remember coming in here."

She smiled. It was gentle and dreamy. "And I don't remember getting under the covers. I know I should be offended, but you're far too comfortable. Remind me to get angry later."

He chuckled. "Absolutely."

She scrubbed her nose into his chest and threw her arm over his stomach. He decided he was going to burst at any second.

"You know what, Wade Mackey?"

"Tell me."

"You are the sexiest man alive."

"Well, thank you."

She lifted her head. "I'm going to regret that."

"I know, but I don't mind."

"This is where I tell you to get out of my bed, isn't it?"

"Probably," he said honestly, kissing her forehead, "but I was hoping you wouldn't."

"Okay, I'll save that one for later, too." She shifted closer to his side, closing the one or two millimeter gap between them. "I think I'll go back to sleep now before I have to be logical and reasonable and this lovely dream is spoiled.''

"Excellent idea.''

To his surprise, she did. After a few moments her breathing returned to the deep, steady breaths of sleep. He wished he could do the same....

Leah awoke and noted the barest hint of sunrise through the gap in her curtains. Her head was on Wade's chest, and remembering her short conversation with him at some point during the night, she supposed she really hadn't moved. Her subconscious wasn't stupid. Lying with him like this was worth any amount of stiffness.

She knew she was a fool. She knew when the light of day hit and reality made an unwanted intrusion, she would have to think about all the things she'd shoved into a corner of her mind. But for now, just for a while, she wanted to enjoy this sensation of utter contentment. It was a wonderful experience, no matter how transitory.

It was as though some deep part of her understood this feeling would never come again, that somehow her responses were brought forth by Wade alone and would never be recaptured when they parted company. Her life was too busy and he lived too far away for her to pretend they would see each other again.

The inevitability of the parting made her heart hurt, but she wasn't so foolish as to dream of what could never be. She was not the woman to keep Wade happy forever. He needed someone compatible with his world. And just as she didn't fit such a role, neither would Wade be compatible with hers.

But, having leashed her panic of losing control again, she was determined to listen to the beating of his heart without regret. She rubbed the side of her nose where the wiry hairs on his chest tickled her. The muscles under her hand rose and fell with his breathing, his skin taut under her hands. She hadn't thought of a man's skin feeling silky, but Wade's was. It was smooth and hot, and Leah had to restrain herself from letting her fingers play across the surface of his stomach, to tangle in the triangular-shaped patch of hair that narrowed from his broad chest into a thin line that disappeared beneath his jeans.

He seemed so deeply asleep she decided to take the chance and indulged in one light stroke up his stomach and over his chest, across his shoulder, down his arm and then back to his waist. A strong, callused hand caught hers.

"You probably shouldn't do that," he said, his voice strained. "I'm not complaining, mind you, just warning."

"I'm sorry." She felt uncomfortable for the first time.

"Please, don't be. Just know that I've held you in my arms most of the night, and my restraint is at the breaking point."

She tried to roll away, but his arm kept her firmly in place.

"Don't go. Not just yet."

"It's morning. We should—"

"No, we shouldn't. Let's just pretend the moon's still out and you can talk sexy to me again."

Leah felt her face flame.

"I thought that was impossible." His voice was a rumble in her ear.

"What?"

"To feel someone blush. I think you just set fire to my shoulder."

She pinched what little skin she managed to grab on his stomach.

"Ouch!"

"Then stop! I can't help it."

"I know, that's why I love to tease you. The blood rushes to your cheeks, and against the pale smoothness of your complexion, it makes you look all innocent and precious."

Innocent and precious. There were two words she'd never heard used to describe her. Oddly, she liked them, and she liked who had said them to her.

Wade kissed the top of her head and ran his hands down the back of her robe. "I want to make love to you."

"I know."

"You sound rather unconvinced."

"Not at all. I'm just tired of feeling scared, Wade. Of being on guard. I keep telling myself that I won't lose control the way I did last night. Night before last. Whatever. I actually believe myself for a minute or so."

"Tell me what you're so afraid of, Leah."

Leah was silent for a long time as she formulated her words.

"How do you sum up a lifetime of experiences in a few sentences? The long and short of it is, I had to become an adult at twelve years old. I wasn't given the option of doing the things I wanted. So while my brothers and sisters got to have crushes and indulge in fantasies, I had to be practical. When my Dad died, and then my grandaddy not long afterward, I decided that loving someone hurt much too badly. It made me quite certain I had to keep my heart safe by staying remote."

Wade nodded slowly. "Would you believe I'm afraid of losing control, too?"

At first she would have said no. Then she considered that he was a tightly contained man and had had to be responsible much younger than most. Of course a loss of control would bother him.

"Then why are you willing to risk it again?"

His chuckle rumbled under her ear again. She decided she liked the way it tickled her cheek.

"Because I've never experienced anything like what we had together."

It was her turn to laugh. "Yeah, right. You can't fool me, Wade. I know your daughter, and I'm pretty sure she wasn't an immaculate conception."

He kissed the top of her head and she felt him smiling.

"True, but I didn't say I'd never had sex. I said I'd never had what I had with you."

"Which is a little difficult to believe. Surely you've had lots of opportunities since your divorce."

"I've had lovers, Leah. In fact, I've been involved with someone off and on for a long time, but even though the sex is good, this is different."

She tried to ignore the searing spasm of jealousy tearing through her. It was absurd for her to be jealous of his other lovers. She had no claim on him.

"How was it different?" She blamed the dim room for her uncustomary boldness.

"I'll only tell you if you'll tell me what you felt."

She didn't think she was up to facing his challenge. "Okay, another question, then. What happens if we make love again? Where do we go from there?"

"I honestly don't know. The only thing I can think of is we're trying to play it too safe. We're being too rational, trying to apply logic to something that defies reason. It's kind of like falling off a horse. You don't think about it, you just get up and get back on or you'll never ride again."

She absolutely, positively refused to indulge in the sexual connotations of his statement.

"It's still risky," she said.

"All of life is risky."

"Uh-oh. I think we just switched to the psychology track. Do we really want to go there?"

"You tell me. You brought the subject up."

His hand was gradually drifting lower and lower as he

rubbed her back in slow, sweeping motions. Any second now his long reach was going to allow him to caress her hip and backside and she was going to be lost.

She shifted away and propped herself on her arm. She could see his face in the slash of sunlight streaking into the room.

"I'm not sure I can do this," she whispered. "What if I risk the mountain with you and then I fall off?"

Wade propped himself up and leaned forward to place a soft kiss of promise on her lips.

"Then I'll catch you."

Nine

Leah closed her eyes and concentrated while she still had the chance. The last time she'd listened to the urging of her soul, she'd ended up a basket case and looked more foolish than she ever had before.

But like the tempting call of the siren, the urge to feel innocent and precious once more was stronger than the warning to play it safe. She hated her tendency to analyze everything, but she knew if she looked into the stormy gray depths of Wade's eyes, she'd be lost in the tide threatening to overwhelm her.

Bless his heart, Wade probably thought he was containing his desire, keeping his needs, his wishes, from persuading her...

How little he knew about his power. How oblivious he was to his ability to move her. His unconscious command over her senses scared her as much as, if not more than, her loss of control when they'd made love. If Wade had been the culmination of a purely sexual fantasy, she probably could have dealt with the aftermath, but Wade touched her much more deeply. He called to the lonely part of her wanting a partner, a mate. The part she had never been able to completely exorcise, or to completely convince she was better off alone.

Slowly opening her eyes, Leah watched him watching her. Oh, she was a thousand times a fool, but she would take this risk. And if she fell and he couldn't catch her, well, she'd deal with the damage later. After all, what more could happen now? She'd already exposed her soul.

Pressing forward, she kissed him. Slowly, languidly. Tasting him again, scratching the bristles of his beard, stroking the planes of his chest.

Wade needed no further invitation. She savored each touch, shivering as he slipped her robe from one shoulder and kissed a trail of fire down her collarbone and into the hollow of her throat.

There was no urgency, only a desire to know each other. Long moments passed of pure exploration and deep, drugging kisses. Tantalizing, seeking, exciting touches. His hands mocked the modesty of her robe, and he finally swept it from her, leaving her aching for him as he slipped off his jeans. Those lonely seconds before his body returned were torture, but the moment his heated skin slid against hers, she sighed.

This time he loved her slowly, each movement, each thrust one step building on another with such promise she was both delighted at the enticing wait and eager for the culmination.

He didn't rush the trip. Instead, he took her with him on a tour of ecstasy. There was no other word for the overwhelming lightness of being, of fulfillment, of utter completeness, that took her over entirely.

When their release came, it did so powerfully, beautifully, the perfect ending of a time spent in paradise. They clung to each other long after their bodies had finished shuddering.

Wade moved his weight from her, but nestled her closely against him, and she snuggled into the curve of his arm. He pulled the light sheet over them and they rested in the cool room, avoiding the sunlight slicing across the corner of the bed.

Leah wondered why she wasn't falling apart. She'd lost control just as easily this time as the last, for there was no doubt her will had been just as helpless inside her need. Surely, after what she'd just experienced, she'd be willing to do anything to keep Wade with her.

But she couldn't avoid the truth. The wedding would be over soon, and then they would have nothing to keep them together. She wasn't going to give up her career, and Wade wasn't going to give up his ranch. At one time she might have been happy with long-distance or sporadic relationships, but she knew a now-and-again relationship with Wade would never be enough for him...or her. She'd tasted more than passion in his arms. She'd experienced joy, a wholeness, and bits and pieces of this heaven would never be enough. If she allowed her heart to sway her, she would never be able to stay away from him.

No, ending their relationship cleanly was much safer for her sanity. The separation would be easier if they claimed this moment, cherished it and parted good friends. He would always have a special place within her, forever hold a part of her.

"I can't believe I never asked you."

Wade's question startled her.

"Asked me what?"

"If you were protected. I'm sorry, Leah. I guess I keep forgetting things are different these days."

Leah patted his stomach. "I know these modern times are hard for you, but don't worry."

He shook his head, his hair rustling against her pillow case. "You know, dating is too much trouble."

"For whom? You, or the lady?"

"Both, actually. I mean, aren't you supposed to get a blood test before you even kiss somebody nowadays?"

"Probably, but it's hardly practical."

He stroked his fingers down her arm, making her shiver. "So how come I don't need to be worried for you?"

"I've been on the Pill since I was in college."

He stretched his neck so he could look down at her. "Really? Is that safe?"

"As safe as anything these days."

"Have you thought about having children?"

"Oh, when I was in my twenties I played with the idea. But the fact is, I was practically a mother at twelve, raising my siblings. In my own way, I've done a version of the mothering thing, and I never wanted anything to interfere with my plans."

"Do you still feel that way? Any regrets?"

She shifted onto her elbow and looked down at him, lovingly tracing his collarbone with her fingernail. "You want to know the truth? The first time I've ever felt real regret that I haven't had children was when I was helping Myra Jo choose her gown. I looked at her and had a moment of incredible sadness come over me. I will never have such a time with my own daughter. But otherwise? No."

He stayed silent and Leah wasn't sure if she wanted to know what he was thinking or not.

"I can understand," he said finally.

"You can?"

He nodded. "I know how caught up I get in my work. Why should you be any different?"

Once again he managed to flabbergast her. If there was

any type of man she was sure would be unwavering in his belief that all women wanted children, it would be a cowboy.

"Now Jonathan," Wade continued, not noticing her silence, "is a man meant to be a father. When that boy finally settles down, he'll probably have a dozen."

Leah chuckled. "You act as if Jonathan is a teenager, always calling him a boy."

"He's eight years my junior, and I had to do a lot of his raising when our dad got sick. I can't help that's how I see him."

She snuggled down and rested her head on his shoulder. "What about you? You're young, too. Do you want more children?"

"Oh, if it happened now I wouldn't mind, but I wouldn't even consider it when Myra Jo was younger. She had a rough enough time with a single parent. I wasn't about to make her feel second place by adding a stepmother and stepsiblings."

"She might have adapted quite well."

"And she just as easily might not have. I wasn't going to take the chance."

"You are a stubborn man, Wade Mackey. Has anyone ever told you that?"

Sweeping her onto her back, he kissed her quite thoroughly. "A few folks, but especially one certain curvy brunette."

She wrapped her arms around his neck and pulled his head down for another kiss. And another.

Some small part of her mind heard the telephone ringing, and heard the machine on her night table click on. Whoever it was could just wait. Wade's lips were much more important.

Myra Jo's voice coming through the speaker sent Wade rolling off one side of the bed as she bolted off the other.

"Leah? This is Myra Jo. I'm looking for my dad. If you talk to him or know where he is, would you ask him to call me at Penn's? Here's the number..."

She looked at Wade, who had already slipped on his jeans while she had grabbed her robe. They shared an embarrassed smile. How ridiculous of them to behave like teenagers caught necking, but Myra Jo had now done it to them twice.

"Do you mind if I use your phone?"

"Not at all."

Determined not to listen, she went to the bathroom and started the shower. She let the hot water pound her delightfully sore muscles as she lathered herbal shampoo into her hair. By the time she had conditioned it and bathed her skin with the new shower gel she'd purchased, Leah assumed Wade had had plenty of time to finish his call. She wrapped a towel turban style around her head and belted a terry robe around her damp body.

Wade was dressed and sitting on the couch when she entered the living room. Since he had his hat in his hand, Leah assumed he was about to leave.

"Is everything all right?"

"Yeah. She just wanted to be sure I still loved her."

"She's just nervous, Wade. Don't be upset with her."

"I'm not."

The agitated movement of the hat was a dead giveaway that he wasn't finished. She sat down a cushion away from him and rested her arm on the back of the couch.

"You smell delicious," he said, looking her over with appreciative eyes. "And look as sexy as all get-out."

She'd never thought of a bathrobe as sexy, but the man was entitled to his opinion. "Thank you. Now tell me what's wrong."

He took a deep breath. "Would you go shopping with

me?'' he asked quickly, as though if he didn't say the words fast enough he wouldn't say them at all.

"Shopping? Um, of course. What for?''

"A tuxedo.''

Leah sat up straight. "Really?''

He nodded.

She cocked her head to the side, threatening the curled towel's precarious perch. "Why? Why now?''

"Because I've been doing a lot of thinking. I honestly hate suits. They feel like straitjackets. But I finally figured out the tuxedo isn't the real problem.''

"And what caused this revelation?''

"You.''

"You're kidding.''

"No, I'm not. You told me how hard it is for you to let yourself lose control, and I understand. Then it hit me. I've been doing exactly the same thing, and if you had the courage to risk being with me this morning, my wearing a tuxedo seems rather paltry by comparison.''

"But the two issues aren't the same.''

"They're not? Wearing a tuxedo, to me, meant dancing to someone else's tune—just because they said it's the right thing to do.'' He harrumphed. "Whoever the hell *they* are.''

"Yes, but my choosing to be with you had nothing to do with someone else's opinion. It was wholly my issue about—''

"—giving up part of who you are. Compromising your rules.''

She thought for a moment. "I guess you're right, but I never would have made the connection.''

"Leah, I chase stupid, stubborn cows for a living. When I put on a tuxedo, I feel like I'm playing dress up.''

"So what changed your mind? Why this particular moment?''

"I'm running out of time.''

Still lost in his thoughts, Wade continued, "You know, I don't give a flying fish who else is in the church. My daughter wants this, and I'll oblige her." His voice choked. "I guess I fought so hard because some part of me knew when I put on that tuxedo, I was going to lose my baby. I must have figured if I just didn't wear one, the wedding would all go away."

Tears filled Leah's eyes. "Oh, Wade, I'm so sorry. I had no idea how much it hurt for a parent to see their child marry."

"Not hurt, exactly. Well, yes, but not...oh, hell. I don't know how to explain. I know she's not falling off the edge of the earth or anything, but things will be different between us."

She put her hand on his shoulder and squeezed. "Well, this we can take care of. By the day of the wedding, you'll have the best-fitting tux this side of New York."

He nodded and took her hand in his. "Thanks, Leah. I really appreciate it."

She patted his wrist. "It's my job, remember?"

She didn't wait for a reply as she headed for her bedroom. Looking over her shoulder, she said, "There's plenty of fruit and bagels in the kitchen. Why don't you grab a bite while I dress."

Once back in her bedroom, Leah placed a hand on her stomach to calm the butterflies. What was she going to do? There was no use denying she was crazy in love with the guy, not with the way her heart had reacted as he'd talked. Not with the way her pulse had gone crazy when she'd looked at his dark head and heard the pain in his deep voice.

As she dried her hair, she worked on convincing herself she had to be cool, had to act normal. Never in her wildest dreams could she have a man like Wade; it would never work, even if he was so inclined. In her mind, the man had as much as said he'd like more children. After all, he was still young.

She'd worked with enough couples to know ambivalence usually meant yes. Wade might *say* he didn't care one way or the other, but the fact that he hadn't made up his mind was the same as wanting another child. He just wasn't acknowledging it.

Leah couldn't look at herself in the mirror. She didn't want to see the agony reflected in her eyes as she considered how much it would hurt to learn he had married and was going to have a child. She didn't want another woman to have him, but neither could she tie him to someone who couldn't give him a child, nor be the kind of wife he wanted. It wasn't that she wasn't able to have a child. She was unwilling, which would be much worse to a man such as Wade. Her momentary thoughts of a baby didn't equal a total change of heart.

She told herself she didn't have to worry about anything today except getting Wade fitted for a tuxedo, get through the rehearsal when it came, and then manage to stay together during the wedding. After that, she was free. Rhonda would supervise the reception, so she only had to last two short weeks before everything was over and she could collapse into a puddle.

Pulling her hair back into a stylish clip, she dressed in casual slacks and a knit pullover, adding comfortable sandals instead of heels at the last minute. Wade was munching on a pear when she waved to him down the hall before disappearing into her office. She counted the seconds until he appeared in the doorway to watch her as she sat behind her desk. She enjoyed the sensation as she looked up the number to her favorite tailor and made the call to set an appointment.

In retrospect Leah decided two weeks was an incredibly short amount of time. She hadn't seen Wade since the afternoon they'd ordered his tuxedo. Her days had been manic and her nights long and lonely. He would call, and the sound of his voice would nearly bring her to tears. She should be grateful their schedules had kept them apart, but her heart didn't agree that it was proof that forever wasn't an option for them.

Finally the day of the rehearsal came. She could hardly bear the long hours until Wade picked her up. She'd never had a client chauffeur before, but Wade had insisted.

For the first time in her entire career, Leah appeared at an event in casual attire, and she had done it for Wade. Her only regression from his request had been to twist her hair into a simple roll and secure it. Otherwise, she looked much as she had the day they'd gone shopping.

She was waiting when he pulled up outside her door.

"Hi, beautiful."

"Hi," she said shyly. She couldn't help but feel bashful at the look in his eyes.

"Ready to go?"

She climbed into his truck and he pulled her into the middle seat, close against him. She admitted to feeling awkward, thinking she was much too old to be sitting with him like a prom date or something. She ignored his smug smile when she didn't scoot back, though. Her discomfort was worth being close to him.

Once they reached the church, the business at hand quickly took her away. It helped that she simply had to concentrate. She conferred with the photographer, the organist and the soloist. She shared a conspiratorial smile with Tammy Griffen, and continued her checklist.

Soon it was time for the run-through. Leah moved to the vestibule and hugged Myra Jo and Penn. "Are you ready?"

Myra Jo looked tired, so Leah reassured the nervous bride that everything was going perfectly.

"Thanks, Leah. I really appreciate all you've done,"

Myra Jo said. "And...I'm...I'm really sorry for being so ugly at the barbecue. I wanted to tell you in person how bad I feel about the way I acted."

Leah reached over to stroke Myra Jo's chin with her thumb, wishing she could wipe the gray smudges from under her eyes. "Don't worry, sweetheart. I've forgotten all about it. Now, you just go back and wait with your dad while I line the attendants up. Don't worry about a thing."

At her signal, the organist began Wagner's traditional wedding march, and the bridesmaids made their way down the aisle at a uniform pace.

Wade struggled with the emotions rampaging through him. When he looked down at his little girl, gazing toward her intended, he was forced to face the fact that he wasn't the center of her life anymore. He didn't want to keep her a child—she was grown up now—but his heart still hurt to let her make such a big step without him.

He still felt she was a jumble of spitfire and fragile porcelain. She was so quick to take on the world, yet her shoulders were so tiny. Would she and Penn be strong enough to help each other grow? They were so young and hadn't been battered by life's trials yet.

Wade looked down the aisle at the man his daughter was staring at. He confessed he'd been harsh on the boy, and he regretted it now. He made a vow to find a way to apologize, because there was no doubting Pennington loved his little girl. That made up for a passel of faults, or at least the faults a daddy perceived.

Wade felt a sadness, deep and hollow, take over his insides. How different his life would be after tomorrow.

His gaze slipped to Leah, and the feeling intensified. Once the festivities were over, she'd be gone, too. Until this moment he hadn't acknowledged how much his existence had been measured by whether or not he'd see her. On the days he'd known she would be showing up, his heart had been light from the moment he'd gotten out of bed. Even with all they'd gone through, the thought of not having her in his life left him bereft.

On one hand, he wished Leah wasn't so stubborn, but then she wouldn't be the Leah who had stolen his heart. Yet, if she weren't, he might be able to convince her they could find a way to be together. He knew she considered the wedding their last moments together. In a funny way, it made sense. All the obligations he'd put on hold would come crashing in on him next week, and he was sure Leah's next wedding would take as much of her time as this one had. He doubted she would find a solution to their scheduling dilemma. After all, he couldn't see one, either.

Myra Jo's tug saved him from further ruminations. He looked down at her, hiding his thoughts, as they slowly walked down the marble aisle. They had barely made the halfway mark when Myra Jo stumbled.

"What—?"

Wade caught his daughter just as her eyes rolled back in her head, and she slumped to the floor.

"Myra Jo," he cried frantically as people came running from all directions. "Baby! Talk to me!"

When she lay silent, he looked up, and the first thing he saw was Leah's anxious face as she knelt beside him.

"Call a doctor!" he shouted. Noticing the people crowding in, he snarled, "Get back so she can breathe."

Everyone complied except Pennington. He knelt on Myra Jo's other side and took her hand, placing his fingers against her wrist and looking at his watch.

Wade wanted to yank Myra Jo away from him, but managed to keep his cool and remember that Penn had finished his residency. Even so, Wade didn't feel he was experienced enough to practice on his daughter. Then he felt a flash of sympathy as Penn struggled to keep a calm facade as he checked her pupils and felt her face and neck.

"Her pulse is stable, and her pupils are responsive. Her skin is clammy, but I don't think—"

"Oh, my head," Myra Jo whispered, lifting a weak hand from Penn's grasp to rub at her forehead.

"Just lie still, honey. You fainted."

Myra Jo opened her eyes and saw her father holding her and Penn kneeling anxiously at her side. "I fainted? You're kidding. I've never fainted."

Wade managed a rough smile. "Well, you did this time, kiddo. And you scared the hell out of me."

"I'm sorry, Daddy. Penn. I didn't—"

"Hush," Penn said softly, wiping a damp tendril of hair off her forehead with shaky fingers. "We're going to take you to the hospital and get you checked out. I don't think there's anything serious, but we're not taking chances."

Myra Jo struggled to sit up. "Don't be silly. Just get me some water and I'll be fine."

"Over my dead body," Wade informed her in an even tone.

Myra Jo looked over his shoulder. "Leah, help me out here. Tell them to let me up."

Leah shook her head. "Not a chance, sweetheart. You just about gave us all heart attacks."

Myra Jo huffed, but didn't argue further. Leah watched as Myra Jo tried to stand, and both men reached to slide their arms under her knees. Leah's eyes met Myra Jo's, and they shared a smile at the sight of the two men nose-to-nose over her legs.

"Son, I know she's yours as of tomorrow, but today she's still my little girl."

Penn matched him look for look before reluctantly moving away. Wade stood, hefting his daughter into his arms and it scared him witless to discover she hardly weighed more than a good saddle.

Wade had already started walking toward the door, Penn

at his side, when he turned to see Leah, strain tightening her face.

"Come with me?" he asked.

Relief flooded through him when she immediately nodded. "I'll be right there."

To hell with the job. He wanted her beside him.

He heard her telling everyone to please go home and they would be contacted as soon as possible. Without another word she ran down the aisle and was at his side before they made it to the parking lot.

"Daddy, I can walk—"

"Hush. Don't give me any lip right now."

Wade was obviously heading for his truck when Penn stopped at his sedan. Another eye-to-eye battle occurred between the men, but Wade gave in this time, settling himself with Myra Jo against him in the back, while Penn drove and Leah rode shotgun.

No one complained when Penn tested the boundaries of several speed limits on the way to Seton Hospital, and, by some miracle, the emergency room wasn't overly crowded. It probably didn't hurt that all the doctors and nurses knew Penn. Myra Jo was immediately taken to an examination room.

When he wasn't allowed to go back with her, Wade was fully struck by the realization that Myra Jo wasn't a little girl anymore. He stood there, frozen, until the feeling of Leah's hand on his arm broke through his stupor.

He felt wooden as she led him to two black vinyl chairs in the waiting area.

He was grateful she didn't try to strike up a conversation. He just sat there, her hand enveloped in his, while he studied the speckles in the tile at his feet. After a moment he put his arm around Leah's back and drew her to his chest, needing to feel her against him—solid, real, close.

Other than a curt nod of acknowledgement, Wade didn't

say a word when the senator and his wife hurried in and took seats across the way. Leah wasn't surprised to see Tammy right behind them, along with two other of the bridesmaids, but they, too, seemed to understand the need for solitude. They took chairs near the Bradfords and talked quietly among themselves.

The forty-five minutes before Penn reappeared through the double doors felt like forty-five years. He hurried forward, motioning everyone to stay seated.

"They ran an EKG and her heart's fine. Dr. Atkin says he thinks she's just dehydrated and worn out. Nothing too serious. She'll be okay."

Leah felt relief flood through Wade, and the whole waiting room seemed to heave a sigh of thanks. She was also touched when Penn put a comforting hand on Wade's shoulder. Wade gave the young man an acknowledging smile.

Penn continued. "It'll take a while for her blood work to come back and her blood pressure's a bit low, so they're going to keep her overnight and start an IV to get her electrolytes up."

"When can we see her?" Wade asked, his voice hoarse.

"When they get her to a room. Probably an hour or so."

"Can I see her now?"

Penn looked genuinely sympathetic. "I don't think so. They're pretty busy finishing up so they can transfer her upstairs." He tried to grin at his future father-in-law. "She said to tell you to stop pacing a hole in the floor."

Wade's attempt at a return smile failed, but he clapped his hand on Penn's shoulder to let him know the effort was appreciated.

"I'm going to go back," Penn said, standing. "I'll come out every few minutes and let you know where things stand, okay?"

Wade nodded and watched Penn's retreating back with

a mixture of irritation and envy. He knew he shouldn't be
angry at the boy; after all, he was a doctor. But he wanted
to be the one at Myra Jo's side. He'd always been the one
to make things right before, and he didn't want some young
punk taking his place now.

"She's fine," Leah said softly, caressing his jaw to make
him turn his head toward her. "Stop worrying, Daddy."

Even for Leah, he couldn't dredge up a smile. He took
his arm from around her and stood. "I need some air."

Leah watched him go outside, aching for him, hating her
inability to help. She was even more amazed at Senator
Bradford. Except for common courtesies, he had kept his
mouth shut.

Mrs. Bradford caught Leah's eye. "We're so glad she's
all right. We've grown to love her, and I'd just—"

She choked off her words and fought back tears. Leah
saw Mrs. Bradford for the first time. For that matter, the
senator as well. He was obviously deeply worried, and his
lack of speech was more indicative of his distress than any
words he could have uttered. Mrs. Bradford's hands were
trembling as she searched her purse for a tissue.

Leah knew some of Wade's fears could be put to rest
now. Whatever machinations Senator Bradford might be
planning, he appeared truly concerned. It was clear Mrs.
Bradford was looking forward to having Myra Jo for a
daughter-in-law and if they just remembered that in the
future, things would work out fine.

Leah was indescribably glad.

She offered the Bradfords an encouraging smile. "You
wait for Penn. I'll go talk to Wade."

Leah found him outside on one of the wooden benches,
his forearms braced on his knees and his fingers clasped
together. His face was so forlorn, she felt her heart clench.

She sat next to him and put her hand on his thigh. "Hi."

He turned his head to place a kiss on her forehead. "Hi."

"You okay?"

"I guess."

"Want to talk?"

"I'm not sure."

She rested her head on his shoulder. "Well, you just let me know. I'm here."

He took a deep breath and released it slowly. "Thank God."

"Amen," Leah said. "She's going to be fine."

"No," Wade said, shaking his head. "I mean thank God you're here."

She lifted her head, startled. "What?"

Wade scratched the side of his neck. "You're the only person I could tell right now that I feel like a damned fool."

"Wade, you didn't have anything to do with—"

He jerked to his feet and paced a tight, angry circle. "I had everything to do with it! I'm the one who tried to get her not to marry Pennington. I'm the one who dragged his feet. I'm the one who stressed her out so badly she collapsed at her own rehearsal. It is my fault. It's *all* my fault."

Leah stood up with her best, no-nonsense posture. "Wade, stop it! Right now. Sit down and listen to me."

Surprisingly, he did.

"Now listen, buster, you may have been a contributor, but this is not all your fault. True, you've been stubborn, but no one, and I mean no one, loves that girl as much as you. I'm not making light of him, but even Penn hasn't loved her long enough to love her as much. You were doing what you thought was right."

"That doesn't mean—"

"It means everything. You aren't the only one who has been yanking on Myra Jo. If you're going to throw blame around, throw some on the senator, some on her mother," Leah's voice grew ashamed, "and some on me."

"On you? What are you talking about?"

"I'm just as guilty of putting the spotlight on the event and not the couple. I needed this wedding to be a success for my business. I even told Tammy to keep her pregnancy a secret so no one would get distracted before the wedding. I'm not proud of myself for being worried about how this wedding would reflect on Brides and Babies. I just hope Myra Jo will forgive me." Leah stared off toward the helipad. "And I hope you will, too."

"Leah, that's ridiculous."

"No more than you taking all the blame. And maybe I can say this because I'm not a parent, but Myra Jo deserves some blame, as well. She hasn't been taking care of herself, and she let everyone manipulate her at some point or another. She's going to have to get tough if she's going to make it in this marriage."

She could see Wade struggling with an affront at her words, but she wouldn't take them back even if she could. Everyone had to take responsibility for their actions, even tiny, delicate Myra Jo. Leah already loved her more than she cared to admit, but she wasn't blinded by a parent's protectiveness.

She was afraid for a moment she had put an unbreachable wall between her and Wade. Then the blaze faded from his eyes, and he finally nodded. "You're right. Much as I've been denying it, she's a big girl now. I still feel like a total heel, though."

"Oh, I'm sure Myra Jo will let you make it up to her. But the first thing she'd want is for you to stop beating yourself up."

He nodded, suddenly weary. "Let's go back in and see if Penn has any more news."

Penn only had time to give one more update before Myra Jo was moved to her room. Wade bribed the Auxiliary lady who was just locking up the gift shop to let him purchase the biggest stuffed bear they had and a vase full of flowers.

Tammy and the girls were thoughtful enough to leave without seeing Myra Jo. They asked Leah to give their friend their love, and Leah thanked them. She hurried to catch up with others headed for Myra Jo's room, and was once again amazed when the Bradfords waited for Wade to precede them inside. Penn was already there, on the far side of the bed, holding Myra Jo's hand.

She smiled when she saw her father. "Now here's a welcome sight. My daddy bearing gifts." She giggled. "No pun intended."

He gave her the bear, put the flowers on the nightstand, and bent over the rail to kiss her cheek. "Of course not." He looked her over carefully. She seemed so small, lost against the white sheets, the IV paraphernalia a startling intrusion at her head. He was comforted that her face had regained some color.

"How are you feeling?"

"Fine, just as I told Penn I was feeling fine, and just as I'll be saying for the next heaven-knows-how-many times."

The Bradfords stood side by side at the foot of the bed, holding hands and wearing grateful expressions.

Leah moved to Wade's side. "I'll make all the calls, Myra Jo, don't you worry. You just get well and we'll reschedule everything as soon as you're up to it."

"If you so much as make one phone call, I'll never forgive you," Myra Jo said solemnly.

Leah stared at the young woman who, at that moment, was very much her father's daughter.

"I'm only going to say this once," Myra Jo said, making a sweeping look around the room to be sure everyone was listening. "I'm getting out of here in the morning. At two o'clock tomorrow afternoon, I'm going to be at Church of the Rock in my wedding dress and if you all aren't there, as well, I'll never speak to you again. Do you understand?''

Five heads nodded their silent agreement. None of them was foolish enough to say anything otherwise, not with the warning glances Myra Jo was giving out.

Wade chuckled. ''I guess I don't have to worry about you sticking up for yourself anymore.''

''What?'' Myra Jo asked, turning away from Penn.

''Nothing, honey. You just go to sleep and I'll pick you up in the morning.''

''I'll let everyone know you're all right,'' Leah added. ''I'll meet you at the church early tomorrow, okay?''

Myra Jo nodded, suddenly fading after her burst of energy. It probably had as much to do with the sedative a nurse shot into her IV solution as sheer exhaustion.

The Bradfords said their goodbyes, but seemed reluctant to leave. Leah watched, fascinated, as Wade squared his shoulders and walked purposefully over to Senator Bradford. The two men eyed each other and Wade held his hand out first. Leah held her breath until the senator put his palm firmly against Wade's and the two men shook hands as equals for possibly the first time.

The Bradfords left, and Penn followed Wade and Leah to the door. Handing Wade his keys, Penn said, ''You go ahead and take my car. I'm going to stick around until all the test results are in. I'll get a buddy to drive me home.''

''Thanks, son. Call me if there's anything…''

''I will. But don't worry. I'm sure everything is going to come back fine.''

Leah's condo was closer than the church, so it made sense for Wade to take her home first. The closer they came, the more weary Leah felt. In the aftermath of the adrenaline-filled afternoon, on top of everything else going crazy in her life, Leah was sure her reserves were depleted. She was grateful that all Wade requested of her as he stopped by her front door was a hug and a promise that she would go straight to bed.

"I promise, as soon as I make these phone calls."

"Why don't you let me," Wade offered. "You're tapped out."

"No more than you are. Besides, this is my job, you know."

"I'd really like to help."

She squared her shoulders and shook her head. "I'll see you tomorrow at the church. Don't forget your tux."

"Yes, ma'am."

She smiled at his attempt at meek agreement.

He seemed as reluctant as she to break eye contact, but eventually, feeling a bit awkward, she headed inside.

Wade drove to the church and parked Penn's car in the covered parking lot behind the Fellowship Hall, knowing Father Jim wouldn't mind in this circumstance. He walked back to his truck and headed home...feeling very lonely.

Ten

Leah closed the door to the bride's lounge behind her, amused from Tammy Griffen's efforts to pay back Myra Jo with a gentler version of the teasing she'd received just a year ago.

She found Wade outside, leaning against a giant oak that was far older than the church itself.

"You're doing great," she said to get his attention.

"Pardon?"

"Keeping that tree up. You're doing a great job."

"Well, someone had to do it."

She rested a shoulder against the trunk, facing him. She didn't have a real reason to be out there. She just needed to see him. Despite the multitude of things keeping her busy, she found herself searching for him constantly, as though to reassure herself he was still around. Which was crazy, of course, but Leah couldn't cast away a feeling of impending disaster. Not where the wedding was con-

cerned—everything was moving flawlessly. But rather,
where she and Wade were concerned. She felt they had so
much left to say to each other, and by the time the wedding
was over, it would be too late. And now, with the wedding
at hand, there was no time to be alone with him. Standing
outside and leaning against a tree didn't count. Not with
the guests beginning to trickle in.

Jonathan came out and joined them, catching Leah by
the waist and pulling her to his side for a hug. "Hey, beautiful, is this shindig about to get started?"

She smiled at him and disengaged his arm. Jonathan's
sweet talk was just to goad his big brother, of course, and
she appreciated Jonathan's attempt to distract Wade. Not
that she minded being flirted with by a man as handsome
as Jonathan, but her pulse tripped at a different Mackey's
attention.

Jonathan's happy smile suddenly dimmed as he looked
across the parking lot. His expression caused Wade to look
backward, and she had to stretch to see what had prompted
the rather caustic change in both men's expressions.

The answer was easy. Julie had arrived, with her husband
in tow, wearing an outfit by a designer Leah knew well.
Leah also knew the dress probably cost more than Myra
Jo's whole ensemble. Somehow, though, she doubted Julie's clothing had upset Wade.

Before she could ask any questions, Wade abruptly
pushed away from the tree and headed in Julie's direction.
She couldn't help but notice, despite the tense moment,
how incredible Wade looked in his tuxedo. Jonathan was
hardly a step behind him, and even from the back, the two
Mackey brothers were libido stirring.

Wade and Jonathan met Julie before she entered the vestibule. They were too far away for Leah to hear what they
were saying, but she was sure Wade was informing Julie
about the fainting spell. When she tried to brush past him,

Wade caught her arm in a none-too-friendly grip, while Jonathan's support kept Julie's husband back a step. Wade released Julie, but from the look on his face, Leah was sure even Julie wouldn't be stupid enough to ignore the warning he'd given.

Leah followed as they went into the church, seeing Julie head for the bride's lounge. Leah headed in that direction even before Wade sent her a look and a demanding jerk of his head. She couldn't stop her professional eye from making sure all the ushers were escorting in the arriving guests before she turned her attention to Myra Jo's mother.

"Mrs. Carollton," Leah said pleasantly to stall her so they could enter together. "You look fabulous. Nikonos, isn't it?"

Caught off guard, Julie lost her initially hostile expression and smoothed the lapel of her fitted jacket. "Yes, it is." She looked at Leah closely for a moment. "You're the little wedding lady, aren't you?"

Leah refused to take the bait. "As a matter of fact, I've had the pleasure of working with Myra Jo for the happy event." She reached for the doorknob. "Let me get this for you."

Ignoring Julie's raised brow, Leah went into the lounge and let the door close behind them. Myra Jo was on the chaise lounge in her foundation and slip, wisely waiting until the last second to put on her petticoat and gown. She looked much better today, but no one was going to let her dress and stand for any longer than necessary. The photographer was taking shots of the church and would be back any moment to do the usual bridal poses.

"Oh, baby," Julie gushed, hurrying over to buss Myra Jo's cheek with an air kiss. "You look just beautiful."

Julie was correct. Myra Jo's makeup was flawless, and her hair had been done in a herringbone French braid that had taken nearly an hour to complete. The style was not only elegant, but would keep the long, dark tresses in place under the veil.

Myra Jo rose to her feet. "Thanks, Julie. You look pretty spiffy yourself."

Leah kept a straight face when Julie's lips tightened.

The bridesmaids had all lowered their voices and cast sidelong glances at Julie. Leah took the time and tension building in the room as cues to get things rolling.

"It's time, girls. Let's get dressed."

She didn't wait to be asked for help. She started with the first person in her vicinity and assisted each of the tall, thin women into their gowns without mussing their hair or snagging their slips on the zippers. When Julie left the room, Leah immediately moved to help Myra Jo into her finery.

When the photographer came in to take his candid shots, Leah returned to the foyer. She was headed in Wade's direction until he shifted his stance, and she saw the woman he was talking to. With nothing to base her guess on but pure instinct, Leah knew this was the lover Wade had talked about.

She was so stunningly pretty that Leah's stomach began to churn. The woman looked like a young, but even prettier Sophia Loren. Tall, dark headed, svelte figured, self-assured. She was smiling up at Wade with a look of intimate affection. She radiated confident sexuality and success.

Leah hated her.

Then she calmed herself. Now was not the time to become a green-eyed monster and attack a woman she didn't even know.

Wade seemed to sense her presence and turned. He motioned her over, and it took every bit of training and experience Leah had to put a pleasant smile on her face as she moved forward.

"Leah," he said, slipping his arm around her waist, "I'd

like you to meet Ysabel Franciotti, a long and dear friend of mine. Ysabel, Leah Houston.''

"Delighted to meet you," Ysabel said in a captivatingly accented voice, holding out a hand graced with long fingers and perfectly manicured nails. She looked at Leah intently, her smile fading just a bit before returning even more brilliantly.

Leah fidgeted under the other woman's stare. She felt as though she'd just been sized up, evaluated and tested, and she didn't particularly like the feeling. Yet she also felt she'd somehow passed the exam.

She wanted to hold on to the feeling of animosity that had overwhelmed her a moment ago, but Ysabel was smiling in an open, friendly manner, and her handshake was genuine.

"Likewise," Leah said, amazed at her pleasant tone.

"You have done a marvelous job. Everything is *bellissimo*. I cannot believe I nearly missed the occasion."

Wade interjected. "Ysabel just got back yesterday from Italy. She's been visiting her family."

"How wonderful! I've always wanted to travel," Leah said. "And Italy has been on the top of my list for years."

"Oh, yes, you must come." Ysabel's voice became animated. "There is nothing like my country. I wanted my Wade to come with me many times but I'm sure you know, he will not leave his Texas unless kidnapped."

Wade laughed and looked at Leah. "She says this when she's just finished telling me she has fallen in love with some nefarious Romeo over there and is leaving me forever. That really makes me want to go overseas now!"

In love? With a man from Italy? Leah's heart lightened several degrees, especially in view of Wade's obvious happiness for his old…friend. There was no hint of hurt in Wade's voice, and his eyes sparkled in the Italian woman's direction.

Leah felt a bit disoriented. She had just decided she would never be able to take Wade from a woman as beautiful and polished as Ysabel. Of course, Leah wasn't planning on *taking* Wade anyway, but faced with a flesh-and-blood rival, the incongruity of her thoughts didn't matter. Now she knew the woman was no rival after all, and she felt inordinately relieved.

Ysabel hooked her hand in Wade's arm, and Leah felt another stab of dark emotion. She wanted to yank Wade away from Ysabel, regardless of her long-term relationship with him.

"I must go take my seat now," she said, patting Wade's hand. "I will kiss my girl's cheek at the reception and save my news for when she gets back from her honeymoon." Then she turned her attention to Leah. "Maybe you can make your first trip to Italy with Wade to attend my wedding, yes?"

Leah felt more, much more, than a simple inquiry in Ysabel's question. It was all too confusing.

"Thank you for asking. And, best wishes to you."

"Thank you, *cara.* You are sweet. And I really go this time. You take good care of my Wade, yes?"

Leah tried to find her voice. "I'll...um...do my best."

Jonathan came forward and took Ysabel's hand, escorting her to a seat behind his parents. Earl looked handsome in his slightly dated but well-fitting suit, and Joleen looked adorable in her grandmother-of-the-bride dress. Wade's parents were still exchanging hugs with Ysabel when he touched Leah's shoulder.

"How's everything going?"

Leah jerked herself out of her stupor.

"Just perfect. The photographer should be about done with his shots in the bridal lounge. I'll go check."

Wade stopped her. "Leah, what's the matter?"

She wanted to brush his question off, but her thoughts

and emotions were too raw, and had taken her completely by surprise. "You didn't tell me she was so beautiful."

By the look on his face, her response was obviously not what Wade had been expecting. "Ysabel?" He looked into the church and then back at Leah. "Was I supposed to?"

She closed her eyes and pressed her fingers against her tight forehead. "Yes. No. I don't know. I was jealous when you told me about this woman who was so close to you, but I never thought...I didn't want...I'm just stunned."

Wade appeared thoroughly confused. "Leah, I'm sorry. I never thought about talking about her with you. She's a friend of my whole family, and I told you we've been...close...off and on over the years. I—"

"You don't owe me any explanations, Wade. Especially at a moment like this."

"But you seem so upset."

"No, not upset. Just confused. Thoroughly confused. But I have to put all that aside for now. I must go check on Myra Jo." After signaling the organist to start the prelude, she left Wade before they could continue their conversation.

Years of methodology allowed her to completely shut her raging thoughts away, and she acted as if nothing untoward had happened as she entered the bridal lounge once more.

She took Myra Jo's hand and smiled at her as the organ prelude came through the overhead speakers. "Ready?"

For the first time all morning, Myra Jo looked nervous.

"Hey," Leah cajoled, "you've been cool as ice up until now. Don't get all fluttery on me at the last minute."

"Yeah," Tammy Griffen said, moving next to her best friend and giving her a careful hug. "You wouldn't let me throw up at my wedding, so I'm not letting you toss your cookies at yours."

Myra Jo laughed, as Leah had hoped, and the color

flushed back into her cheeks. "Well, let's get out of here so I won't have as much time to think about it."

Leah led the way out. She hurried to a vantage point which would allow her to see Myra Jo's face when she saw her father.

And Leah wasn't disappointed. When Myra Jo looked across the foyer and saw Wade in his tuxedo, a cry of joy escaped her lips. Heedless of decorum, she lifted her skirts enough to free her feet and practically flew into his arms.

"Oh, Daddy, I love you so much. Thank you."

"Just for you, sweetheart. Just for you." He kissed her forehead. "I'm sorry I was such a horse's behind."

She leaned back in his arms and tossed him a cheeky grin. "That's all right, Daddy. I wouldn't have recognized you if you'd acted any different."

"Saucy wench," he muttered.

Leah hated to break up the happy moment, but the organist was just about to finish his last selection. She looked behind her and found the girls lined up and waiting for the well-known chords from *Lohengrin* to ring out from the pipes.

Jonathan startled her by coming up beside her to pull her hand into the curve of his arm. "Ma'am," he said, dipping his head. "Bride's side, I believe."

Leah resisted. "Jonathan, stop fooling around."

"I'm not. You and I are the last ones up the aisle before the march begins."

She felt a blush furiously heating her face. "Stop it this instant. I can't be in a pew, much less sitting with the family. Now go!"

The distinct, composure-destroying scent of him reached her just before Wade's voice came warm and quiet against her ear. "Unless you want to cause a scene, my dear, you'd better go with my brother. We're not moving a step until you're seated."

She closed her eyes in agony. "Wade, you don't know what you're asking. I'm honored, truly, but you can't."

His lifted brow reminded her how foolish her statement was.

"Please," she begged, anguished tears in her eyes, "don't do this to me."

"Leah," Myra Jo broke in, "we all want you up front. You've become so much a part of us, I couldn't stand it if you had to be 'just the wedding planner' now that we've actually made it to the final moment. Please, do this for me."

Outnumbered and outmaneuvered, Leah put a nervous hand to her hair, checking the simple French roll.

"You look delicious," Wade said against her ear, making her blush for a different reason altogether.

With a determined breath, she took Jonathan's proffered arm and tried to ignore the curious stares she received as Jonathan took her to the first pew. The only odd thing he did was enter the pew first so that his mother was on his right and Leah was on the left, with an open space remaining for Wade.

She could feel Julie staring daggers into the back of her neck from the second pew, but Wade must have put the fear of God into the woman, for she hadn't made the slightest scene when she and Redford had been escorted to the second pew.

Leah put it all out of her mind as the girls made their way down the aisle to take their places along the outside of the communion rail. Pennington waited, as handsome and nervous as every groom should be, and Leah smiled in delight when his face took on an expression of awe at his bride's entrance.

The congregation stood as Myra Jo began her journey. Leah felt tears building as she watched. The tiny woman was enchanting as she stepped confidently beside her father.

But once Leah's gaze slipped to Wade, it stayed fixed there. There was so much in him that drew her. He looked so proud, so fierce. When he let go of his little girl and kissed her, Leah felt a tear slip down beside her nose. She'd seen more weddings than she could count, and yet, she was delighted to discover she wasn't as jaded as she'd thought she'd become.

When Wade stepped back and put Myra Jo's hand in Penn's, Leah smiled, yet her happiness was tinged with sadness. Wade's face revealed little of his thoughts, but Leah knew what he was feeling. No one else might be able to, but she could read the mixed emotions in the depths of his cool, gray eyes. When he sat down beside her and grabbed for her hand, Leah willingly let him squeeze the daylights out of her fingers. She knew he had no idea how tightly he was holding on, but she didn't care.

The rest of the ceremony was a blur. Leah could hardly believe it when Father Jim was telling Penn to kiss his bride and then introducing the new couple to them all. She clapped and watched as Penn and Myra Jo led the procession away from the altar.

Wade offered Leah his arm. They were the first to follow the happy couple, so she didn't know if the Bradfords were right behind them, or Julie and Redford, but Leah didn't particularly care. For the first time she put her trust fully in Rhonda and the rest of her crew and let go of controlling the finale.

Wade kept her close by his side during the photographs and other business that had to be taken care of before they headed to the reception. She didn't mind. She liked the feeling of his arm settled comfortably around her waist, of her hip resting against his. She didn't even argue when Myra Jo and Wade insisted she join in some of the pictures. She felt a bit awkward at first, but she would cherish these shots in the years to come as a reminder of a very special time in her life.

The only thing she absolutely refused to do was be included in the receiving line at the reception. She won this round with Wade, although he wasn't particularly pleased. Leah teased him about only wanting her there so he didn't have to stand next to Julie, but she knew it was more than that.

Which was exactly why she was so determined to get away for a moment of quiet.

She was touched by each of Wade's impulsive moves. They were so much a part of him, yet were something rare for him. He had been, and still was, so wound up he probably didn't realize how inappropriate some of his actions had been. But then again, knowing Wade, he wouldn't have cared.

Did he know what he was doing to her heart? Did he realize his sweet gestures made her fall even more deeply for the one man she wanted to love but could never have? Leah wrapped her arms around her waist as she stood alone outside the country club. The light wind was welcome in the still-hot hours of the early evening, and she let herself be mesmerized by the sight of the flowers in the landscaped area dancing in the breeze.

"Say there, missy. How come you get to skip out of the zoo?"

Leah jumped and worked to calm her startled heart as she turned to face Mr. Mackey. She tried not to let her face reveal he was about the last person she would have expected to see.

"I'm playing hookey. I'll be right back in."

The elder Mackey chuckled, and Leah could easily see that Earl Mackey had been just as much of a lady-killer as his sons were.

"I wouldn't, if I didn't have to."

Leah nodded in understanding. A silence settled between them, making her want to fidget. She knew Mr. Mackey's presence was no accident, so she wished he would say what was on his mind.

"What I can't figure out," he finally said, appearing to search the horizon intently, "is which one of you two is the bigger fool."

"I beg your pardon?"

"You or my son."

Leah had just enough humor to tease. "Jonathan? He's young, but I don't think he's a fool."

Mr. Mackey's ice blue eyes crinkled in amusement. "Well, him, too, but the older boy's the one I worry about more. That boy's the stubbornest cuss I've ever met."

She tried her best to hide a smile. "I can't imagine where he gets it from."

A gruff-throated chuckle acknowledged her shot. "Must be from his mama."

"Mr. Mackey—"

"Girl, I'm not one for nosin' in on anybody's business so I'm going to say what's on my mind then get back to the party. My years have given me a little wisdom. Not much, I'll admit, so you don't have to say it."

He cast her a sideways glance, and she gave him a wide-eyed look in return.

"I always hoped Wade would get together with that sexy Ysabel. They weren't all over each other like kids, but they had a good friendship, which isn't a bad place to start a marriage." He looked at the flowers before clearing his throat. "Anyway, from the first moment I saw you and Wade together, I knew my plans for the boy would never come to pass."

Leah stayed silent, not about to jump into this train of thought.

"Well, Ysabel and I've been talking in there," he said,

jerking his head back toward the club, "and she says a man'd have to be blind not to see that you and Wade love each other. But she thinks from the way you were looking at Wade during the wedding that you have some crazy idea about giving him up."

He cocked his jaw to the left and rubbed his chin. "I like that little woman, but she sure does come up with some whoppers sometimes. Just jumps to thinking things from out of nowhere. Must be because she's Eye-talian or some-thin'."

"Mr. Mackey, I appreciate—"

"I ain't done, girl. Just let me finish."

Leah had never intentionally been disrespectful to an elder in her life, so she did as instructed.

"I won't say much more, but let me tell you something my pappy told me. He said, 'Boy, I done a lot of things over the years, some good and some bad. But the only ones I've ever regretted was ones I didn't.'"

Earl Mackey turned to face her and put a hand, showing signs of age but still carrying strength, onto her shoulder.

"Don't do something you'll regret, girl. The good Lord only gives us a few chances at happiness. My Joleen was smart enough to hang on when I was a jackass. Don't do like me and nearly lose something you can never get back." He took a deep breath. "I ain't plannin' on leaving this earth anytime soon, but I want my boys happy and settled before I pass."

Without another word, he walked back into the reception.

Leah had to sit down on one of the wooden benches placed before each pillar. She was stunned as she replayed Earl Mackey's words over again in her mind.

She sat there far longer than she'd intended, trying to sort out her confusion.

"So this is where you ran off to."

She smiled and closed her eyes, leaning sideways into Wade's chest as he slid onto the bench beside her.

"Just for a minute. I was coming back."

"I'm not complaining," he said against her hair. "This is the first moment we've had alone all day."

"And the last..." She cleared her throat to regain her voice. "Until the wee hours of the morning, anyway."

They rested together, despite knowing they should be heading inside.

"Don't leave me, Leah."

She shrugged out of his embrace and gave him a puzzled look. "I'm not leaving."

His smile was sad. "That's not what I mean, and I think you know it. Don't draw away from me tonight. You and I both have been thinking about the future, and I want to leave tomorrow until tomorrow. Please?"

"Wade, pretending isn't going to change anything. We—"

"Don't pretend, then. *Want* to be with me tonight."

"I do want to," she whispered. "Heaven help me, I want to."

"Don't make me lose my baby and you in the same night."

"That's dirty pool, Wade."

"I'm a desperate man. I think I'd do pretty much anything to keep you with me right now." He held out his hand. "Let's go back inside and watch my baby in her glory. We'll be mostly ignored now, anyway."

He was right, of course. And there was never any doubt she'd give in.

The spotlight was on Penn and Myra Jo, as it should be. Wade took a moment in the bright light when he cut in on Penn at the appropriate place during the first song. After dutifully dancing with Mrs. Bradford, the bridesmaids and even Julie, he rejoined Leah at the table.

They sat together, not talking, just watching the goings-on with their hands clasped under the table.

Myra Jo and Penn finally left. Leah felt Wade had come to a semblance of peace as he hugged his daughter. And, to Leah's delight, his handshake with Penn contained much more than mere courtesy.

With the newlyweds gone, Wade and Leah were free to leave. Saying good-night to their tablemates, they stood to go. She was too numb to be shocked when Earl Mackey hugged her, and to feel more than confusion when Ysabel gave her a conspiratorial smile and wink. Leah gave her head a little shake to clear it as Wade led her away.

A glance at the dance floor made her stop short and draw Wade's attention there.

"Would you look at that?" she whispered.

Off to the side, in a shadowy corner, Jonathan and Rhonda were dancing. If you could call the stranglehold they had on each other, with barely a sway, dancing.

Wade smiled. "Well, whadaya know."

"Rhonda said she and Jonathan went to high school together."

"Yeah, but I don't remember him dating her."

Leah shook her head. "No, I don't think they did. But I'll tell you a secret, if you promise not to tell."

He agreed solemnly.

"Rhonda had a huge crush on Jonathan."

Wade chuckled. "Well, it looks like the flame might not be dead."

Leah turned around and pulled Wade with her. "I just hope she knows what she's doing. I don't want her to get hurt."

"She's a big girl, Leah. She can take care of herself."

Leah didn't voice her opinion that even the strongest of women stood little chance against a Mackey seduction.

But Rhonda wasn't foremost on her mind. Wade was.

And how much it was going to hurt in a few minutes when she kissed him goodbye.

"Thank you," he said as they reached her car. "For what you did for Myra Jo, for me. Everything."

"You're welcome. This is the most special wedding I've ever done."

Cicadas chorused around them in a low buzz that built to a crescendo and faded. Grasshoppers sang to each other across the darkness. June bugs cast themselves against the lamplight far overhead in futile fury.

Leah almost laughed. She'd never thought about insects much, but in this moment she sort of understood them. Mr. Mackey's words came back to haunt her, reminding her not to self-destruct her chances for happiness. She forced the voice away.

"I wish you'd go home with me," Wade said matter-of-factly. "I'd like to keep you in my arms all night and bury myself within you until we're both so exhausted we can't move."

"I know."

"Is that I-know-yes or I-know-no?"

She put her hands on either side of his face and looked deeply into his eyes. "It's I-know-yes. If you want me tonight, Wade, I'll give myself to you, for you. But you have to acknowledge tomorrow will only be harder."

He pulled her against him and held her so closely she could hardly breathe. Of course, she wasn't especially concerned about breathing at the moment.

He kissed her slowly and then let her go. "I don't ever want you to be with me unless it's one hundred percent your wish as well."

"Oh, I want to be with you that much. And more."

They only spoke with their eyes as they drove to Leah's condominium. Wade didn't release her hand for an instant.

Once inside, they embraced and stayed locked in each

other's arms. They held on to each other, absorbing the other's essence, willing time to stand still. Eventually Wade reluctantly set her away from him.

"You need to get out of those clothes."

She gave him a half smile, and nodded.

"And into something comfortable. Like a pair of sweats or something."

Leah frowned, puzzled.

"Leah, we both know I'm not going to ask this of you."

She looked into his eyes for a long moment before finally nodding. "For all your bluff, the one thing you can't deny is your deep-bred sense of fair play. You wouldn't make love to me tonight because you know you'd just be trying to dull your sense of loss. Which wouldn't be fair to me."

He smiled at her insight. "You're right, of course. But it doesn't stop me from wanting you. And to assuage a hurt isn't the only reason I'd make love to you."

"I know," she said again, her smile returning broader this time. "But one more night together won't make things better in the long run."

"This is where we tell each other we can't see each other anymore, isn't it?"

Her smile faded to sadness as she met his eyes and nodded. "We're too different, you and me."

"Or maybe too much the same?"

She shrugged, not resisting when he pulled her down onto the couch and back into his arms.

"I'm not sure I can live without you, Leah."

"And I don't know if I can live without you. But what I do know is eventually you and I wouldn't be able to give what the other needed." She snuggled her head into his shoulder. "From day one, you made a point of letting me know no one is going to change you. Unfortunately, I'm as pigheaded as you."

"You think I'd—"

"Wade, would you honestly be happy with me living in Austin and rarely available because of my career?"

He sighed and pressed her head back down on his shoulder. "No more than you would be with me two hours away at the ranch. And I can't up and leave cantankerous cows any more than you can cantankerous brides."

"And babies."

His laughter rumbled against her ear. "And babies."

Thinking about babies hurt too much. Of all the reasons they couldn't be together, that was probably the most important of all. Wade was ambivalent about having a second family someday. As he'd said, he was still a young man. She couldn't risk him changing his mind. She couldn't bear watching his love fade and resentment build as he realized what he had given up. The one thing she was absolutely, unequivocally sure of was that she wasn't going to start having babies at this time in her life.

She finally broke the silence. "We're not going into my bedroom."

"All right."

"We're not going anywhere near the bedroom."

"All right."

"Did you hear me? I said—"

Wade kissed her into silence. "I heard you."

"Good," she said breathlessly. "Then you take the comforter off the top shelf in the closet and make us a pallet on the patio. I'm going to change."

Her fingers trembled as she put on cotton stretch pants and an oversize T-shirt. She was an idiot. Or maybe lunatic was a better word. Yes, she decided, lunatic was a much better choice. She was going to call her mother in Washington State tomorrow and find out if insanity ran in their family.

When she joined him outside, Wade's jacket and tie had been discarded, and the two top buttons on his shirt were wrenched open. She had no idea where his cummerbund had been thrown.

He was stretched out on the pallet, using the cushions from the lawn furniture as pillows. Leah was sure she'd never seen a more gorgeous pair of tuxedo slacks, especially when worn by a tall, dark cowboy. Even his black, shiny boots, crossed at his ankles—which were perfectly acceptable with formal attire in Texas—looked incredible on him.

She moved beside him as gracefully as possible and rolled to her side to lay her head on his chest. His arm immediately circled her waist and pressed her closer.

"Wade—"

"Shhh. No more talking. Just stay with me and we'll watch the sun come up."

She did as he asked, savoring each second of the early-morning coolness. The moon bathed them in an ethereal glow, and she begged God to let the night last forever.

For all her exhaustion, sleep never occurred to Leah. She wasn't giving up one second of this time with Wade, recording every breath he took in her memory, counting every heartbeat as if it were her own.

But the sky gradually lightened, and bright yellow rays eventually shot over the horizon. She damned the sun, but supposed it didn't have any choice in its course. Just as she didn't.

They finally stood, their movements awkward as they tried to rise while still holding on to each other. Still, the silence remained between them as they walked through her house.

At her door, she pulled him tighter and held on until the muscles in her arms ached. After pulling his head down for a fierce, passionate kiss, she stepped out of his arms.

"Goodbye, Wade."

"'Bye, Leah."

She somehow managed to close the door behind him and crawl into her bed without crying.

In fact, she didn't cry the whole day.

Because a person needed a heart to cry...

And hers was completely broken.

Eleven

Wade thrust the posthole digger into the ground and yanked the chunk of dirt out with a grunt. Camping at the line shack and the hard, physical labor of working on the fence in the fallow pasture wasn't keeping his mind occupied the way he'd hoped it would. He and Jonathan had been working the length of the fence for a week now, since just after the wedding, and they'd hardly spoken two words to each other. Which was fine with Wade. But the job hadn't kept Leah off his mind for more than a minute at a time.

"Women," Jonathan muttered as he dropped a post into the newly dug hole and stalked to the Jeep.

"You can say that again," Wade said as he pulled out another digger of dirt.

He ignored the pain in his shoulder where an old post had slammed into his muscle. He also ignored the myriad cuts, scrapes and splinters. Not that he enjoyed pain, but even after a week he carried some hope that maybe tonight he'd be sore and tired enough to sleep.

"Let's take a break and then clear some brush. Until we do, we've gone about as far as we can." Wade wiped the sweat from his forehead onto his sleeve.

He didn't wait for an answer. Instead, he headed for the Jeep and some water, sitting in the shade cast by the vehicle. Using the tire for a backrest, he looked at the section of fence they'd already restrung, and beyond to the scrubby, rough country. He took a long draught of water and poured the rest over his head. As rivulets ran down his face, he chuckled.

So much for the mystique of the cowboy working the range. The movies made it look as if they rode around all day with their ten-gallon hats pulled close over their eyes. Oh, he'd brought Thicket, one of his favorite cow ponies aptly named for its willingness to brave any thicket for a hidden calf. And Jonathan had brought his favorite mount, since they had a whole section of overgrown brush to haul out and burn. But the truth was, cattle didn't range over thousands of acres anymore. They were systematically moved from pasture to pasture, and modern cattlemen rode Jeeps and helicopters more often than horses. One thing unchanged between the old way and the new, though, was the work remained sweaty, dirty and hard.

And usually he loved it. But this last week had been an exercise in pure routine. His body had worked, doing the chores of thirty years, but his mind had never let up.

Every purple bruise on his body made him think of the alabaster sweetness of Leah's breasts. The scratch of the brambles made him remember the silk and satin of her skin. And at night the stars peeping at him through the unshaded window in the line shack made him swear he could see the twinkle in her eyes when she was teasing him.

Wade wiped his forehead again and wanted to smile, but

he was afraid his mouth was broken for good. He didn't think he'd ever laugh again.

He looked back at the fence and wondered if this was what he really wanted. Was his reputation, his wealth, his success, worth anything without someone to share it with? But if he didn't have his ranch, what would he do with himself?

A long time ago he'd dreamed of traveling the world for the finest bulls and heifers to raise a herd of purebred black Angus. After all, he had the money now to indulge himself, but somehow, a purebred herd had always been a "someday."

He wondered where along the line he'd convinced himself he had no options.

He put his tumbler back into the Jeep and headed over to retrieve his digger. Pulling his hat down on his forehead helped block the sun, but it didn't stop his thoughts.

Leah looked around and cursed softly. Her desk was clean. There wasn't a single file that hadn't been noted or tagged or logged. There wasn't a dress in the store that hadn't been inventoried. There wasn't a phone message she hadn't returned.

She glanced at her clock. It was only midnight. What was she supposed to do now? She could start the preliminary contacts on the three new weddings she'd taken on in the last week, but she doubted any church secretaries or caterers or photographers worked quite this late.

Rhonda was no help. She'd been in a royal funk ever since Myra Jo's wedding. Leah had only risked asking what was wrong once, and she still checked for teeth marks on her throat for her efforts.

But the one thing she absolutely would not do was dwell on memories of Wade. On how he'd looked in his tuxedo pants, pleated shirt and cummerbund. Or how he'd smelled like woodsy spice instead of his usual citrus cologne. Or how his skin had felt like hot silk over solid rock. Or the way his tongue tasted inside her mouth and the way the corner of his lip would twitch when he was trying not to smile.

She stood up and threw her pen on her desk in disgust. Yanking her purse out of the drawer and snatching her keys, she locked up and got into her car faster than should have been humanly possible.

Going home didn't help, though. She only ended up in her home office, her chair swiveled to the window, staring at the sky full of stars.

She had everything she wanted, right? Her business was back on track; after all, the Mackey wedding had earned her the hoped-for reviews. Her broker had called to tell her one of her major stock investments had split, and she had made enough money to retire right now, if she wanted to. But what would she do if she didn't have her business? What did her success matter if she only had her computer to share it with? What else did she want to do? And when had she forgotten how to dream?

Once upon a time, she'd played with the idea of being a travel writer. In fact, she even had a proposal on the computer somewhere. She had planned to send it to the leading bridal magazines to see if one would bite on her suggestion for a running advice and travel column. Every bridal magazine offered such types of articles, but Leah hoped her slant, which added a hefty dose of humor, would spark an interest.

She really wouldn't mind giving up consulting. It would be no hardship to leave dysfunctional and feuding families. Still, her talent drew her to design, and her fantasy included a small, high-quality salon where she created custom bridal ensembles. She wouldn't mind the retail market, but she wasn't going to spend all her energy there. That was why the travel writing went along so well with this scheme. She could travel when she wanted, take custom orders when she wanted and do whatever else she wanted when she wanted.

So, why hadn't she?

Because before now, the thought had been too scary. If she wasn't working every minute, then she was risking her ruin. Now she'd have to be nine kinds of stupid to lose all the money she'd stashed away since she had been old enough to earn it.

And where did all this leave her? Comfortably wealthy, successful, and so lonely she wanted to die. Feeling foolish, she took the tuxedo jacket Wade had left behind out of the closet and slipped the fabric that still carried the smell of him over her body.

She went to bed in her usual nightshirt and lay staring into the darkness. The lack of light didn't help her sleep, and it didn't stop her thoughts.

Wade checked his watch—2:00 a.m.

Well, that did it. He didn't know much after thinking all night, but he was sure of one thing. He loved Leah. He adored her. He couldn't live without her.

He jumped off the cot and started dressing.

"What are you doing?" Jonathan complained from the darkness on the other side of the shack.

"I'm going to go talk to Leah."

"Now?"

"Yes, now. I'm taking the Jeep, but I'll have one of the boys come out first light."

"Okay, but what's got a burr under your saddle?"

"I can't take it anymore. I have to try and convince her we can make it work, somehow."

"You're a fool, Brother. Trying to work things out with

a woman who's as different from you as night and day is plain stupid.''

Wade zipped his jeans and sat down to pull on his boots. He had the distinct feeling Jonathan wasn't talking about Leah.

"Maybe," Wade answered as he turned on a flashlight to find his hat and keys. "But I'm going to try."

What could it hurt? Impulsively tracking Leah down at five o'clock in the morning, which was what time it would be after he got home, grabbed a shower and made it to north Austin, might not be as silly as it sounded. Both of them had been so damned reasonable, maybe insanity was the logical answer.

Minutes later the sound of the Jeep's engine cut harshly into the quiet night.

Leah turned her head and checked the clock. It was almost four o'clock.

Well, that did it. She didn't know much after thinking all night, but she was sure of one thing. She loved Wade Mackey. Adored him. Couldn't live without him.

And she didn't know how, but she was going to go find him and convince him that they could work out their differences. They had to.

Logically, she should call. He might not even be home. But, damn it, being logical was what had made her so miserable in the first place. Using the return of the tuxedo jacket as a painfully obvious excuse, she was going to risk seeing him. Besides, she didn't have anything better to do, and if worse came to worst, she'd have killed four or five hours of loneliness.

Which was better than lying sleepless in her bed.

Untangling herself from her sheets, she dressed in record time and headed to her car.

* * *

Wade checked his watch. Four-thirty. He would hit Elgin any minute. With traffic almost nonexistent, he'd make it to Leah's place in less than an hour.

Leah looked at her dashboard. Almost five. She'd hit Elgin anytime now, and from there, on a nearly deserted highway, it'd probably take her less than an hour to get to Wade's.

She saw a set of headlights coming toward her and flashed her lights. The guy's high beams were stabbing her in the eyes.

The guy didn't respond, but when he whizzed past her, she tested her antilock brakes. Wade!

She pulled a U-turn in the middle of the road so fast she felt like Mario Andretti.

The only problem was, Wade had done the same thing.

She didn't know if she should pull over to the side of the road or what, and then he flashed his lights and turned on his blinker. When he pulled into a deserted parking lot, she was right behind him.

Wade hopped out of his truck and was running toward Leah before she'd shifted into Park. Yanking her door open, he pulled her into his arms like a man dying of thirst reaching for water.

He crushed her to him, covering her face with kisses, burying his hands in her hair, breathing in the scent of her. He couldn't do it fast enough.

He wanted to pull away, to talk to her, but he couldn't. And she wouldn't let him. When he tried, she pulled him back murmuring, "No, more. More."

He gladly obliged until they were both breathless and half-sprawled across the hood of her car. Her legs were hooked behind his knees, and he was pressed into the cradle of her softness, but not nearly close enough.

It took the flashing blue and red of strobe lights to break through their haze of passion. A young voice shouted from behind a bright spotlight, "Hey, you kids. Break it up!"

Leah looked at Wade, wide-eyed, and he stared down at her. Even in the surreal lighting, he could see the wash of red on her cheeks and felt a matching shade creeping up his neck.

"I said get off the car," the voice from behind the spotlight yelled again.

Wade slowly eased off Leah and helped her get to her feet on the ground. When he turned and saw the brown sheriff's car, he groaned.

The spotlight slowly dropped, and he could see the outline of the officer.

"Mr. Mackey? Is that you?"

Oh, dear God. "Yeah, Tim, it's me," Wade yelled back.

Tim reached into his car and turned off the spotlight and the strobes. He walked toward them, fitting his hat on his head.

Wade shifted so Leah was mostly behind him, but as he guessed the stubborn woman would do, she moved right back beside him. Didn't she know he was trying to protect her?

"Mr. Mackey, what in the hell are you doing?"

Tim seemed to realize for the first time that Leah was a woman. "Oh, I'm sorry, ma'am," he said, tipping his hat.

Wade could feel the laughter building inside her, and he could hardly stop himself from busting a gut, too.

"I thought two kids were beating the hell out of—oops, sorry again, ma'am—beating the heck out of each other when I drove by." As if considering something for the first time that was beyond his imagining, he looked at Leah carefully. "Are you all right, ma'am?"

That did it. That just did it. Laughter bubbled out of her, and once she started, Wade couldn't stop himself any longer. They held on to each other as much because they wanted to as because otherwise they'd fall.

"Mr. Mackey? Mr. Mackey! Have you two been drinking?"

The question only made things worse. The second round of laughter sent them both oozing to the ground.

"Wait," Wade gasped, holding out his hand. "Hang… on…just a…second." With considerable effort, he managed to stop laughing by clearing his throat.

"Now, Tim," he said, stifling another chuckle and helping Leah to her feet. "I know this looks strange—"

"That's for damned sure! Oh, sorry again, ma'am."

"I'd like to explain, but it'd take all night. I've been a bit rocky since Myra Jo got married, and this little lady and I had, uh, have some things to work out. We both sorta picked the middle of the night to go find each other."

Tim looked decidedly unimpressed. "What the he— uh—what does that have to do with you two cavorting on top of a car in the middle of a parking lot?"

Wade couldn't help himself. He had to let out another chuckle. Cavorting. He hadn't cavorted since he was… well, hell, come to think of it, he'd never cavorted. "We, uh, were just…glad to see each other, son."

"Well, you should save your…gladness…for a more private place."

Wade was almost ready to get onto the pup for acting so uppity, when he remembered the pup was a man now and had the authority of the law on his side.

"I'm sorry, Tim. Really I am. And I'm most sorry about embarrassing the lady. If you wouldn't mind, we're just a short drive from her house and we'll go…uh…talk there."

Tim nodded authoritatively. "Sounds like a good idea, Mr. Mackey. A da—uh, darn good idea."

Tim left them, almost reluctantly, and Wade followed Leah to her house. They were fortunate Tim had turned the opposite way on the highway, or they both would have earned speeding tickets.

They hardly took the time to shut her door before resuming where they'd left off.

And it wasn't until much, much later they began to talk.

Or tried to, anyway. Leah's breath was still labored when she looked at him and said, "We have to talk."

Wade nodded, taking deep breaths to slow his heart. "I know," he said, bracing his arms on the bed beside her shoulders to relieve her of some of his weight.

But he wasn't moving until he'd had his say. There was no better time than now, while still nestled deep inside her. "I love you, Leah. I can't live without you. I don't know what it will take, but I'm going to make you marry me."

Leah rolled her eyes and met his intense gaze again. She ran her fingers down his chest, catching a trickle of sweat.

"Yeah? You and whose army?"

"I don't need an army. I'll just keep you captive until you acquiesce to my demands."

She pinched his nipple, earning a yelp and disgruntled look from the man poised above her.

"Why don't you just ask me, you sexist jerk," she said with her voice full of coyness and love.

"All right, will you marry me?"

Leah wiggled her hips, nestling his cooling body more firmly between her thighs. "I don't know. Are you sure we're fit for each other?"

Wade growled, deep in his throat, and bent his head to kiss her with a nearly bruising passion. "What do you think?"

"Oh," Leah said, stretching her arms up and then resting her hands behind her head. "I think we'll find a way to manage."

Wade nipped her earlobe.

Leah jumped. "What was that for?"

"You haven't told me you love me."

"Yes, I did."

Wade bent for her ear again.

"Okay, okay! I love you, you big, stubborn cowboy. I love you more than anything, and I can't live without you."

His body defied his age by responding eagerly to the passion in her voice.

Leah's eyes grew wide. "Already? My, but aren't we feeling spunky."

"I'll show you spunky, young lady."

She smiled. "I certainly hope so."

Her smile faded as he moved against her. "Wade, I have to ask you one thing."

"Now?"

"Yes, now. It's about children."

"I thought you said—"

"I know. What I meant was, are you sure about this? I can't give you any children. It's just not right for me, and it's so important to you."

"Who said that?"

"You did."

"Did not," he said in a husky tone.

"You said if it happened—"

"—I wouldn't mind. But I don't care at all if you and I have children. In fact," he said, stroking her slowly to show her he was more than ready to move on, "I don't think I want any distractions from our time together."

Leah saw the truth in his eyes, and the scars on her heart seemed to start healing.

Funny. She'd never believed in miracles before.

"Let's just spend the rest of our lives practicing, shall we?" she asked, sliding her hands down his hips to urge him on with the business at hand.

"Ma'am," he said, nuzzling into her neck, "I'd be happy to oblige."

Epilogue

"Come to Grandma, sweetheart," Leah cooed as Myra Jo placed the one-month-old infant in her arms. The sweet little girl was the most beautiful baby ever born. Leah was sure.

And Wade didn't dispute her supposition. He tried to take Taylor Morgan from her, but Leah made a biting motion toward his advancing hands and he backed off.

"Just think," Leah whispered, placing a kiss on Taylor Morgan's downy-soft head. "You were there when Granny and Grandaddy got married, and we didn't even know it."

Myra Jo and Penn had stood up with her and Wade just weeks after their own honeymoon. Once she'd been convinced Wade wasn't giving up a dream of a second family, nothing could have stopped her from marrying him.

Leah had even accepted some good-natured ribbing from her new daughter about their small ceremony. Only Wade had seemed to understand that after years in the business, the last thing she had wanted was a big church affair. Having Father Jim marry them on the back porch had been just perfect.

Now they had a new grandbaby to play with, and Leah was sure life couldn't get any better.

She and Rhonda had talked, and they'd sold the bridal business. Rhonda kept the "Babies" side since she'd always enjoyed it more. And Leah had been as proud as she'd ever been the day one of the magazines accepted her column proposal. She was now busy writing articles and traveling, and they often combined Wade's search for stock for his purebred Anguses with her trips. Each new place was like a honeymoon all over again.

Myra Jo insisted on telling everyone that whenever she called her dad and stepmom, they were in bed or off seeing the world. She said she had no idea her daddy was so spunky.

Finally relinquishing her precious bundle into Wade's impatient hands, Leah stepped back as Penn and Myra Jo took positions on either side of Wade to help admire the baby.

Leah cast a glance heavenward and thought, You know, I've never been one for praying, but thank You. From the bottom of my heart, thank You for giving me the strength to lose control.

Myra Jo reached out and pulled Leah into the circle.

Wade looked at her over the heads of their children and grandchild. She lost herself in those gray eyes, and her world was complete.

* * * * *

Bestselling author

JOAN JOHNSTON

continues her wildly popular miniseries with an
all-new, longer-length novel

The Virgin Groom

HAWK'S WAY

One minute, Mac Macready was a living legend in
Texas—every kid's idol, every man's envy, every
woman's fantasy. The next, his fiancée dumped him,
his career was hanging in the balance and his future
was looking mighty uncertain. Then there was the
matter of his scandalous secret, which didn't stand a
chance of staying a secret. So would he succumb to
Jewel Whitelaw's shocking proposal—or take cold
showers for the rest of the long, hot summer…?

Available August 1997
wherever Silhouette books are sold.

Silhouette®

Look us up on-line at: http://www.romance.net

HAWK

National Bestselling Author

JoANN ROSS

does it again with

NO REGRETS

Molly chose God, Lena searched for love and Tessa
wanted fame. Three sisters, torn apart by tragedy,
chose different paths...until fate and one man
reunited them. But when tragedy strikes again,
can the surviving sisters choose happiness...with
no regrets?

Available July 1997 at your favorite retail outlet.

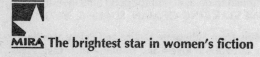

SILHOUETTE®

Desire®

Coming this July...

36 HOURS

Fast paced, dramatic, compelling...
and most of all, passionate!

For the residents of Grand Springs, Colorado, the storm-induced blackout was just the beginning. Suddenly the mayor was dead, a bride was missing, a baby needed a home and a handsome stranger needed his memory. And on top of everything, twelve couples were about to find each other and embark on a once-in-a-lifetime love. No wonder they said it was 36 Hours that changed *everything!*

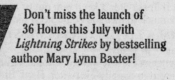

Don't miss the launch of
36 Hours this July with
Lightning Strikes by bestselling
author Mary Lynn Baxter!

Win a framed print of the
entire 36 Hours artwork!
See details in book.

Available at your favorite retail outlet.

COMING NEXT MONTH